JUST FOR KICKS

Judy Dearborn Nill

JUST FOR KICKS Copyright © 2011 by Judy Dearborn Nill. All rights reserved. With the exception of quotations for review purposes, no part of this book may be reproduced, scanned, or distributed in any printed or electronic form without written permission from the author.

This is a fictional work. All characters, organizations, and events in this novel are either products of the author's imagination or used fictitiously.

Jacket Art by Adam Scott Youngers

For Sue and Willie, who, like angels, don't need to be seen for me to know they're there

With many thanks to all who have read and commented on this story.

Each of you has helped to make it the best it can be.

Chapter 1

Petra Goodwyn watched a hunky olive-skinned boy with a military haircut angle across the walkway in front of her. In spite of the cold March weather, he wore no jacket. His shirt sleeves were rolled to the elbows, his backpack slung over his right shoulder. Wind caught the top of his clipped dark hair and ruffled it. The boy paused to shift his pack and answer his cell phone before opening the door to the cafeteria.

Petra had no idea she'd been staring or that her heart pounded until her friend, Jamie Francis, elbowed her in the ribs.

"Chas LaGuardia," Jamie said, rolling her eyes meaningfully toward the cafeteria. "Taken," she added and bit off a huge chunk of apple.

"What do you mean, taken? I've never seen him before. How can he be taken already?"

Jamie pointed to her full mouth, indicating it would be a while before she could swallow. Petra relaxed against the bench, enjoying a spot of unexpected sunshine. Stray crocuses poked out of the grass at her feet, a shy reminder that even frequent Northwest cloudbursts serve a purpose.

"He's obsessed, that's how," Jamie sputtered at last. "Always busy with the love of his life." She wiped her lips with a paper napkin and looked bleakly at the rest of the apple before tossing it into her lunch bag.

"The love of his life? Do I know her?" asked Petra, her hopes strangely crushed. Like she ever had a chance with someone like Chas LaGuardia.

"It's not a her." Jamie considered a moment. "At least it's not a girl."

"You mean—a boy?"

"Nope."

"What are you saying, that something else—something not human—is the love of his life?"

"Yep."

"What?"

"Keep guessing."

"Animal, vegetable, or mineral?"

"Hmm. I'd have to say animal."

"A dog? A cat? A horse? I know, he's a cowboy, and when he's not at school he wears chaps and spurs." Petra smiled. Actually, she could relate to a cowboy, ten-gallon hat and all. She'd taken weekly riding lessons on a borrowed mount before she got sick. If Petra had had any say in the matter, she'd have lived in the country and owned two or three horses to feed, groom, and saddle up whenever she pleased.

Jamie laughed. "You're not even warm."

Petra cocked her head, frowning first in disappointment at the disruption of her cozy fantasy, then in concentration. What could it be? Ordinarily, she liked puzzles, but Chas LaGuardia was a lot more challenging than the average hot guy she and her best friend speculated about during lunch hours at Belville High.

"Okay, I give." She peered into her own lunch bag and pulled out a peanut butter sandwich. "If he's not taken by a girl—or a boy—and he's not into horses or pets, then what?"

"Master Lee's School of True Martial Arts."

"Martial arts! You mean ti-phoo or kung-doo, or whatever it's called? Like that panda cartoon thing? Like—what's his name—Jackie Chan?"

"Not just any old martial arts, Pet. Master Lee's School of True Martial Arts. Emphasis on the *true*."

Petra hesitated. "I don't get it. The true part, I mean. How do you know so much about it, anyway?"

"I sit next to him in Math for Dummies."

"Don't call it that. You make it sound like you're retarded or something."

"I am, in math. Unlike *some* people I know, who take nerdy classes for fun."

"Now that's not fair. You know I didn't take trig for fun. My advisor recommended it." Petra tore at the plastic cling on her sandwich. Why did she always feel compelled to downplay her academic achievements around Jamie? It wasn't as if her friend had been passed over when gifts and talents were being handed out. Beauty, personality, artistic and musical ability—things for which Petra would exchange math smarts in a nanosecond.

"Anyway...." Jamie sighed. "Believe it when I say Chas LaGuardia is taken, taken, *taken* by this martial arts stuff. I've tried to get him to talk about something else—anything else— but he always shoots me down." A gust of wind snatched the paper napkin off her lap, and she dove for it and missed. Springing off the bench, she chased it to the sidewalk. Her pinkish complexion glowed with health, and her thick reddish-blond hair blew around her head in a riot of disorderly curls.

Petra would kill for hair like that. Her own was an ordinary shade of brown, limp and straight. And the only color in Petra's face came out of a makeup kit. She asked, "How do you know this Chas LaGuardia doesn't have a girlfriend? Maybe he's not interested because he's faithful and loyal to her."

What would it be like, Petra wondered, to have a boyfriend so devoted that even a girl as cute as Jamie couldn't tempt him away? Well, someone other than Derek Bender at church, who'd practically stalked her in seventh grade. Or Andrew Karpasian in last year's English class. Someone she wanted.

"No girl would put up with this guy," Jamie said. "I'm not joking. After I tried all my usual things—you know, flirting, sitting next to him in a miniskirt, brushing against his arm with other parts of my body...."

Petra felt the heat rise to her face and hoped that her cheeks, typically so pale, would have the decency to remain that way. Jamie's superior experience with the opposite sex both fascinated and horrified her. She tried to imagine herself brushing her breasts against a random boy and got a picture of the boy, who had suddenly turned into Chas LaGuardia, whipping around to regard her with her father's solemn eyes and saying in her father's genteel British accent, "I beg your pardon?" The imaginary mixture of Chas and Father Peter—her dad, an Anglican priest and the rector of St. Julian's Episcopal Church—prompted Petra to laugh out loud.

"What's so funny?" Jamie demanded.

Petra smothered her amusement. "Nothing. You were saying

what came next, after the—uh—how you usually get noticed by a boy."

"Well," Jamie said, "Chas showed about as much interest in me as a potted plant, and I wanted to know why. I mean was he blind or something? He became my project for a while. I'd lean across the aisle and ask him what time it was, and he'd say 'two hours and ten minutes to *kata* practice.' Whatever that is. Or I'd ask him what he does for fun, and he'd say 'work out at Master Lee's.'"

Petra zipped the remainder of her sandwich into her backpack. "Come on. He can't be that far gone."

"I'm serious," said Jamie. "Once I asked him for our math assignment and he handed it to me stuck inside a brochure called something like *Master Lee Says Try Harder*. It's about practicing martial arts till you drop dead because it's good for your character. Another time I asked him how he'd done on a quiz. He covered up the score and said, 'I always do better on my tests at the School.' I swear, he capitalized *school* as he said it. He talks about that place like your dad probably talks about his church."

"You mean like it's holy?"

"Totally." Jamie shook her head. "I finally gave up on him. By the way, I think he's training to be an instructor there, or maybe he's already made the grade. He told me he'd be teaching new students when he got his black belt, and guess what blessed event occurred last week."

"The black belt?"

"You got it, genius."

Petra snapped her fingers. "That's it."

"What's it?" Jamie glanced at her watch. "Hey, we'd better get going. Two minutes to Horseman." Horseman, as the kids who'd studied French liked to call Mr. Chevalier, was their history instructor.

Petra grabbed Jamie's arm before she could run away. "You can force Chas to pay attention to you by joining his church—I mean his true school of righteous combat or whatever it is. He'd be your teacher."

Jamie's blue eyes widened. "Are you crazy? You expect me to get hit and thrown around for the likes of Chas LaGuardia? I'm not *that* desperate. In fact, I'm not desperate at all. Why don't you do it, if you're so interested?"

Petra turned aside, stung by the word *desperate*. She knew she'd never be in Jamie's league when it came to boys. She would always be a straggler, a timid also-ran. But a new thought made her brighten, and she looked back at her friend. "That's not such a bad idea," she said. "I used to be pretty athletic. I might take you up on that."

Jamie, finger-combing her hair as she and Petra headed inside, stopped abruptly. "Hey, Pet, I didn't mean it. I know you couldn't—you shouldn't—it wouldn't be a good thing for you to…." Her voice trailed off.

"To stalk Chas LaGuardia?" Petra teased.

"No. You know what I mean."

Petra did know. She'd had juvenile rheumatoid arthritis since she was eleven. Most people wouldn't guess she had it now, because after a couple of rough years in middle school, the disease went into a remission that lasted almost to her fourteenth birthday. And although she'd spent that birthday hospitalized with a high fever and inflamed joints, she gradually improved enough to get off steroids and other immune-suppressing medications, which gave her mouth sores and stomachaches and made her vulnerable to every virus that came along. She managed now with herbal supplements, megavitamins, and a quiet lifestyle.

"Oh, that." Petra waved her hand dismissively. "It's been over two years and I'm still okay. I don't watch what I eat so much any more, and half the time I forget to take all those vitamins and things. Besides, I think—" She broke off to suck in a ragged breath. "I think I'm healed." Quietly and decently healed, she might add. The sort of inconspicuous miracle Episcopalians could appreciate. She didn't usually talk religion with Jamie, who wasn't a churchgoer, but it felt important to make this announcement, as if blurting it out made it real.

"Healed!" Jamie tossed her curls. "Remember, I knew you the last time you wound up in the hospital. You didn't get out of bed for weeks."

"It wasn't that long."

"It sure was. And that happened after you'd supposedly been healed, too." Jamie gave an exaggerated shudder. "You scared me to death."

"It's different this time." Petra felt the urge to cross herself but thought it might be superstitious under the circumstances.

She needed to believe her father's prayers and her grandmother's naturopathic remedies had cured her, and that she would never have to go through such awful experiences again. She was free now of the more severe symptoms of illness, but she couldn't do anything strenuous. Her riding days were over. Soccer and softball, too. Petra's doctor had warned that the stress of heavy exercise could bring on another flare-up which might result in a permanent return of debilitating pain and fatigue. She might even wind up on crutches or in a wheelchair. Sometimes Petra felt like she'd turned into an old lady before her time.

"Come on," said Jamie. "We're late." She gave Petra a little push toward the door. "No more talk about Chas LaGuardia or his stupid school of partial farts."

Petra laughed. "Okay, but I wouldn't mind having him for a teacher. Just for kicks." She emphasized the last words and nudged Jamie's side.

Jamie groaned. "Omigod, Petra, that's so bad."

Petra knew Jamie meant that her pun was lame, but she chose to respond at a different level. "Well, maybe it's about time I tried being bad," she said as she opened one of the double doors and held it for Jamie. A stiff breeze rushed in after them, raising goose bumps on Petra's arms and legs. Other last-minute students surged through the doors and swept past them into the crowd. "I get tired of the same old, same old. You know? I don't see why I can't at least try martial arts."

"Uh-uh. Not on my watch. I won't stand by and let you get sick again."

Petra shrugged. "I don't plan to get sick."

"No one *plans* to get sick, Pet." Someone jostled Jamie, and she did a hop-skip to avoid stepping on Petra's toes. "Look, we can talk about this later. Meanwhile, history waits for no one." She jerked her thumb down the hall. "Onward and upward?"

"Horseward," Petra corrected with a grin, at which point Jamie threw back her head and let out a loud whinny.

In the noise and confusion of changing classes, Jamie's outburst didn't draw much attention, but Petra envied her the boldness to do it without caring what people thought. She wanted to possess that kind of nerve again. Wanted to act more like she did as a child, when she dared to get excited, dared to do risky things. But juvenile rheumatoid arthritis—JRA, the child crippler—stood in the way.

On impulse, Petra tossed back her head and echoed Jamie's whinny. Her friend shot her a surprised look, and a couple of freshmen eyed her like she'd just arrived from Planet Screwloose, but for once she didn't mind. It felt good to throw caution to the wind.

The time had come to break out of her carefully constructed cocoon. Push the limits and see where she landed. After all, she couldn't play it safe forever.

Not when she was sixteen years old and itching to live.

Chapter 2

Petra couldn't get Chas LaGuardia out of her mind. Neither could she put aside the thought of showing up for lessons at his school of martial arts.

She'd never seen Chas before Jamie pointed him out—Belville High was one of the biggest public schools in the state—but in the brief space of time it took her to notice him crossing the courtyard to the cafeteria, she'd witnessed something mysterious and self-contained in his demeanor. Petra wished she'd asked more about Chas, like what grade he was in and how long he'd been at the high school.

Maybe his special confidence had something to do with the discipline of moving slowly and deliberately in practice. She recalled watching a group of people in a park going through a set of rhythmic, fluid motions together. They looked so graceful and serene, not at all like the Jackie Chan movies she'd seen with her little brother. Jackie Chan could knock an opponent senseless with one lightning-swift blow, and he was always leaping into the air as if gravity didn't exist. Were those just camera tricks? Or were he and the park people demonstrating different kinds of martial arts? Could students study only the forms that seemed like dancing, or would they be required to learn self-defense in a martial arts school? She would have to find out.

Deep in reflection, Petra had all but tuned out Horseman's drone. Suddenly, her ears pricked up. The teacher had just said "Jackie Chan" along with something else, and the class responded with a tepid round of snickering. "What'd he say?" Petra leaned forward to ask Jamie, who sat in the desk ahead of her.

"Tell you later," Jamie whispered.

Petra could hardly wait for the period to end. Just as she'd been thinking of Jackie Chan by way of Chas LaGuardia, Mr. Chevalier spoke his name. She hugged this coincidence to herself until the bell rang.

By then Jamie couldn't remember exactly why the action film star had been mentioned. "Something to do with vegetables, I think." She lifted one shoulder in a half-shrug. When Petra threw her a quizzical look, she added, "Doesn't matter, though. Trust me, Pet. Bo-o-o-ring, like everything else Horseman says." She rolled her eyes, and Petra laughed. It didn't strike her so funny when Jamie answered Petra's questions about Chas with unwanted advice. "He's a junior, and he moved here from Arizona at the beginning of the semester, but don't get any ideas."

"Why not?"

"Because it won't do any good. In the first place, the fool has no time for girls. I told you how he ignored me. In the second place, your doctors wouldn't like it."

"My doctors! You sound like someone's mother." Not Petra's mother, though. Catherine Morse would never try to discourage her daughter from exploring anything that interested her. Separated for more than two years from Father Peter Goodwyn, Catherine was an independent woman and she expected Petra to be independent as well, even if some of Petra's choices were not to her liking.

Catherine hadn't tried to hide her disappointment when Petra chose to live with her father after the divorce, but she'd respected her decision. Petra had been recuperating from her last major flare-up of arthritis at the time, and it tore her apart to think of letting either parent go. In the end, she'd stayed with Peter at the rectory because she felt he needed her, while Petra's younger brother Zeke moved into Catherine's condo in downtown Belville. The split had been as friendly as a family split could be, but that didn't mean Petra had reconciled to it. She still dropped hints aimed at getting her parents back together. Her father had grown too solitary, in her opinion, and Catherine worked ten to twelve hours a day without Peter's calming influence. Besides, as annoying as Zeke could be, Petra missed him, too.

"Petra Cat Goodwyn!" Jamie waggled her finger in a mock scolding way, assuming the Irish brogue she'd learned in Drama Club. "I'll give you what-for, darlin', just like your own dear mam. You need someone to reel you in before you make a hash of your life."

"You know my mother's not like that. Neither is Dad."

"All the more reason for me to have your back. Now go home and forget about Chas LaGuardia. You'll be glad you did. You hear?"

Petra saluted. "Yes, ma'am!"

Jamie returned a crisp salute and spun on her heel. "I'm off to be the phantom of the orchestra."

"Wait for me after school in the band room, okay? I need to copy your notes."

"Really? That's a first."

"Don't get excited. I missed Horseman's assignment is all."

"Preoccupied with Chas LaGuardia?"

Petra flushed.

"Mind what I said about that heartbreaker, young lady."

"Oh, go blow your horn."

"FYI, it's a reed." Jamie mimed playing her saxophone.

* * *

Petra puzzled over Jamie's notes. Who'd have thought someone so artistic would have such indecipherable handwriting? "What's this?" She pointed at a line of squiggles that looked like a cross between Arabic and computer code.

Jamie stopped pacing and bent to see. "Beats me," she said, "but I'm sure it's not important."

"Then why'd you write it down? Or try to write it down?"

Jamie shrugged. "You almost done? I got a bus to catch."

"Don't worry, I'll drive you." Petra flipped the page of her friend's three-ring binder and caught her breath. "Whoa! You drew a picture of Chas."

"What?" Jamie hung over Petra's shoulder, staring at the sketch she'd made of a man in pajama-like garments karate-chopping a bunch of broccoli. Jabbing her finger at some doodles around the cartoon, she said, "Notice I scribbled *Chan*, not *Chas*."

"I know that," Petra lied. "I just wanted to see if you're awake. Why's he attacking a bunch of broccoli?"

"Hell if I know. Oh, wait!" Jamie sat down on the stool next to Petra. "Now I remember what Horseman said. We were talking about World War Two, and that reminded him of his summer visit to Japan. He told us about a chef he met there who was so slow, Jackie Chan could chop bricks faster than the chef chopped vegetables. Pretty lame, huh?"

"Do you think they can really do it?"

"Who? Do what?"

"The karate masters. Do you think they can just yell *yeehaw* and slice bricks and boards in half with their bare hands?"

"How should I know?" Jamie yawned. "It's been a long day, and it's going to get longer if I have to walk home."

"I said I'd take you. I don't know why you don't let me drive you home every day."

"Because Metro's such a kick." Jamie rode city transit to and from her mother's apartment near Belville Community College. "I've met some fine college men on that route."

And gone out with them, too, thought Petra, glad that none of those dates had amounted to anything. She feared losing Jamie to a serious older boyfriend. She'd found it hard enough when Jamie went out with boys her own age. Petra always felt jealous and neglected until the romance cooled. Fortunately, her friend was notoriously fickle. "A player," in her own words. Petra couldn't remember Jamie sticking with any boy longer than a month or two.

In the student parking lot, Jamie patted the hood of Petra's sporty red convertible. "You're a lucky bow-wow, you know?"

"Quit making me feel guilty."

"Guilty!" Jamie spread her arms to an imaginary audience. "I suggest gratitude and the girl gets guilt."

"Because you don't have a car."

"Do I need one? *Je suis le Metro*," Jamie declared in an

accent their French teacher had pronounced the best in the class. Too bad she couldn't memorize vocabulary or be bothered with verb conjugations.

"All right, then. Woof. But I don't think you *are* the Metro."

Jamie laughed. "Is that what I said? See, I told you you're the brains of the outfit."

Petra unlocked her car and slid behind the wheel with some effort. The little Italian job was too low-slung for someone with chronically stiff knees and hips, but she loved the way it looked and, even more, the way she felt when she drove it. Light and free, like she could gun the motor and rocket to the moon if she wanted to. The car almost made up for not being able to ride Attaboy, the horse she'd been assigned for riding lessons.

"You okay?" Jamie asked after Petra maneuvered out of the parking lot and into traffic without a word.

"What? Oh, sure. Just thinking."

"About what?"

"Horses, mostly."

"Horses? You've got plenty of horsepower under this hood, girl."

Petra sighed. "I know, but sometimes I miss having a real horse under me."

"I don't. I never did get the hang of riding, even though you made me go to that stupid horse camp in fifth grade. Remember?"

"How could I forget? You got a prize for the most falls off a sawhorse."

Jamie shuddered. "I'm allergic to the hideous beasts."

"How do you know? You never got close enough to find out."

"And that's why I'm alive to this day." Jamie ran her hand lovingly over the dashboard. "Now this baby's another matter. How'd you talk your dad into it?"

"I told you, he didn't pay for it. He can't even afford a new car for himself."

Petra's mother had surprised her with the car after she completed driver's education over the winter. She'd purchased it used from a colleague who'd babied it for years. Catherine, an interior designer for a Seattle firm specializing in corporate clients, also pledged to pay for the insurance as long as Petra maintained her grades and a safe driving record. The grades were easy enough. Safe driving was a challenge. So far she'd avoided hitting other vehicles but had crunched one fender on a support column in the undercover parking at her dentist's office and scraped the other on a light pole in the school lot. Dad liked to joke that Petra's little car had simply turned the other cheek.

"I don't mean that," said Jamie. "I mean wasn't he afraid you'd go wild with boys or something?"

"Go wild with boys? *Moi?*"

Jamie chuckled. "I guess not."

Petra wasn't sure whether to feel flattered or insulted. Although she knew herself to be cautious, it hurt to realize that her best friend considered her hopelessly backward. Her mind wandered to Chas. He'd never met her. He didn't have a clue about her history of illness or her puny experience with boys. His beginner's class would provide a fresh start during which she'd work hard, learn quickly, and impress the heck out of him. One thing would lead to another, and before she could say *Karate Kid*, they'd be friends. Dating, with any luck.

She had begun to mentally rehearse what she would tell her father about taking martial arts lessons when she saw something jolting out of the corner of her eye. "There it is!" she shrieked, slamming on her brakes at the entrance to a strip mall. The driver behind them skidded to a halt and blared his horn. Petra put on her blinker.

"What the freak are you doing?" Jamie braced herself against the dashboard and turned to follow Petra's gaze.

"Master Lee's School of True Martial Arts is here!" A shiver ran down Petra's back. It was a sign. Well, of course it was a *sign*. But it was the other kind of sign, too. First Horseman's story about Jackie Chan, then Jamie's cartoon. Now this. It couldn't all be meaningless coincidence.

"So what? You aren't thinking of going in, are you?"

Petra hadn't been thinking at all, just reacting. But it seemed like a good idea, now that Jamie mentioned it. This way she'd have specific information to give Dad about the health benefits of martial arts practice. "You know I need exercise, but my doctor won't let me do sports or P.E.," she'd say wistfully. *"And what's wrong with walking?"* her father would counter. "It's...it's...." It's what? She'd have to give that more thought.

She pulled up in front of the school and switched off the engine. Master Lee's occupied a suite at one end of the mall. A Starbucks adjoined the school on the left, and next to that was a crafts store. A large black-and-white sign, the one that had snagged Petra's attention, ran the length of the school above the plate-glass windows and glass door. MASTER LEE'S SCHOOL OF TRUE MARTIAL ARTS stood out in bold block letters. In smaller print beneath she read that the school had been founded the year of her birth by "the one and only Master 'Springing Tiger' Lee."

My birth date, Petra thought. Another sign.

"Okay," Jamie said. "You've seen the place. Let's go."

"Just a minute." Petra studied a life-sized photo in the window of an Asian man flying through the air, his feet and hands parallel to the sidewalk. More Jackie Chan style than the steady, grounded movements of those people in the park, but no one could start by flying through the air. The easy, flowing exercises had to come first. If Petra took lessons, she would get to know Chas long before they did anything that could hurt her. She turned to Jamie. "Let's go in."

"Are you crazy?" Jamie slumped low in her seat. "I don't want Chas LaGuardia to think I'm stalking him."

"Why would he think that? You're not stalking him, are you?"

"No, but you are."

"All right. Be that way." Petra opened her door. "I'll be back in a minute."

"Hang on," said Jamie. "If I go with you, will you promise to talk to your doctor before you have anything to do with this place?"

"Of course."

"And do you promise you'll *listen*?"

"Sure, I'll listen."

Jamie frowned. "I don't suppose I could get you to promise to do what she says."

"Jeez, you really think I'm stupid, don't you?" Grabbing her purse, Petra got out of the car and waited for Jamie to shut her door before locking up.

"Not stupid. Obsessed."

"Don't worry. This feels right. I mean it feels right to check it out. Who knows where we'll go from here?"

"Who knows where *you'll* go from here. I know where *I'm* going," said Jamie. "Home!"

Chapter 3

A surprisingly familiar odor greeted Petra when she stepped inside Master Lee's school.

Jamie, pushing in behind her, stopped to sniff the air. "Get a load of that."

"Why are you whispering?"

"Why are *you*?"

It was the smell of incense and the extreme quiet. They reminded Petra of a church sanctuary. Her father's church in particular. There was even a bouquet of white silk flowers on a table in the entryway. On the wall above the flowers were framed pictures of Oriental writing. Petra leaned close enough to read some of the English translations. EARN YOUR HAPPINESS. PAIN IS SHORT, PLEASURE LONG. FOCUS. NOTHING IS IMPOSSIBLE. She didn't grasp the meaning of the pain saying, but it seemed vaguely wise. She smiled at NOTHING IS IMPOSSIBLE. That was right out of the Bible. "Nothing is impossible with God." The Gospel according to St. Luke. Dad would be pleased.

"It looks like Master Lee's taking a coffee break," Jamie

said.

"You think he drinks coffee?"

"He must get wired on something to do that." Jamie twisted toward the life-sized cutout in the window, designed to be viewed from either side. From here, the figure of the flying man appeared to be headed straight for a doorway to the right of the entrance. Rows of black plastic beads hung from the top of the door frame almost to the floor.

The beads parted and out stepped a short, paunchy Caucasian man in a belted black outfit trimmed in white. He had a hooked nose and a military haircut similar to Chas's. Petra guessed him to be fifteen or twenty years younger than her father, who'd turned fifty-one on his last birthday.

"Can I help youse?" The man favored them with a smile which didn't reach his deep-set, hooded eyes. A long scar over the left eye caused his lid to droop at the outside corner. His accent, which to Petra's ears sounded broad and nasal, seemed more Bronx or Brooklyn than Belville.

Petra hesitated. She'd been expecting the man in the photo. "Master Lee?"

"Seattle Area Associate Head Instructor Todd." He raised his right hand, and Petra stuck out her own, quickly withdrawing it when she saw he did not intend to shake hands. Instead, he pointed to the photo in the window. "That's Master Lee."

The man gazed raptly at the grainy blowup with an expression on his face of—what, Petra wondered. Pride? Admiration? I know, she decided. Reverence. Worshipful reverence. Something she had seen only occasionally at St. Julian's, most notably when parishioners did the Stations of the Cross on Good Friday. Everything Jamie had said about Chas's devotion was true of this man, too. Petra let what she hoped might be a respectful silence lengthen before she spoke again. "Could we see Master Lee?"

Seattle Area Associate Head Instructor Todd jerked his head around and stared at her. "What? He ain't here."

"Oh. Well, when will he be in?"

The stocky man's face darkened. "Who are you, and whaddaya want?"

"Nothing," Jamie answered before Petra could reply. She grabbed Petra's arm and herded her to the entrance. "We're leaving."

Petra shook her off. "Wait a minute. I didn't mean to offend you, Mr. Todd. I only wanted to talk to whoever's in charge about taking lessons."

"Seattle Area Associate Head Instructor Todd," he corrected. "I'm in charge here."

"Okay. It's nice to meet you, Seattle…uh…Associate…." Petra started to put out her hand again, thought better of it, and dropped her arm. "I'm Petra Goodwyn, and this is my friend Jamie Francis. Is Todd your first name or your last?"

Seattle Area Associate Head Instructor Todd's mouth twitched. Whether with amusement or annoyance, Petra couldn't tell. "First," he grunted after a pause.

"Do we call you Todd, then? Or do you have a last name?" Too late Petra realized her mistake. "I mean, of course you have a last name, but what is it?"

"Call me Seattle Area Associate Head Instructor Todd." He nodded toward the beads. "C'mon into my office." He led them through the curtain to a small, cluttered cubicle. File folders, business forms, and empty Dixie cups littered the desk, some of the cups crushed or tipped on their sides. A wastebasket overflowed with fast food takeout bags.

"Seattle Area Associate Head Instructor Todd?" Petra repeated with a nervous giggle. "Isn't that kind of awkward? What if someone needs your attention right away? You know, in case of a fire or something."

"Shhh...." Jamie hissed in her ear. "You're digging yourself deeper."

The man did not respond. He directed them to a couple of chairs next to a tall metal cabinet and squeezed around his desk to seat himself. Displayed on the wall behind him were two flags, one American and the other unknown to Petra. It featured two sets of slanted parallel lines on either side of a red and blue sun.

Seattle Area Associate Head Instructor Todd tilted his chair back against the wall. "Where did you hear of Master Lee?"

The girls exchanged glances. Petra didn't know if it would help her cause to involve Chas or not. "Well," she began, stalling for time. "We—"

"How old are youse, anyway?" he interrupted.

"Old enough," Jamie snapped, jumping to her feet. "I'll wait for you in the car, Petra."

"Keep your seat," ordered the head instructor. He gestured impatiently until she sat down again. "Old enough to drive, then. You got jobs?"

"I don't," Petra admitted. She hesitated to speak for Jamie, but her friend seemed frozen in place after allowing the man to boss her around. "Jamie used to work as a barista. She's between jobs now."

"Barista?"

Clearly, Whatchamacallit Todd wasn't from Seattle, no matter what his title said. Next door to a Starbucks and he didn't know the first thing about coffee! Should she tell him that *barista* was a fancy name for an espresso server? Probably not, Petra thought, settling back into her chair. Jamie shot her an incredulous look, but she too remained silent.

Todd heaved himself forward and plucked a pencil off his desk. "So who's gonna pay for the lessons?" he asked Petra. "You ain't got your old man waiting in the car, do you?" He leaned across his desk to peer out the window.

Petra suppressed an impulse to offer her services as a grammar coach in lieu of payment. The man talked like he never made it to high school. Maybe that's why his title meant so much to him. Seattle Area Associate Head Instructor Todd—an intimidating tongue-tangler, with or without cue cards. In her mind, Petra had already shortened the clumsy honorific to SAAHI and pronounced it to herself as *Sawhee*. Sawhee Todd. She hoped she would remember what the initials stood for when she needed them.

"Well, can youse pay or not?"

"We have money," Petra said. "What kind of martial arts do you do here?"

"True martial arts."

Petra groaned. She should have seen that one coming. "I mean," she persisted, "is it self-defense or is it—" She broke off. Now what was the name of that thing they did in the park? And where else had she seen it? Oh, yeah. A TV commercial.

"Is it what?" SAAHI Todd jiggled the pencil between his fingers.

"Is it tai-tai—oh, you know, what they do in the ad for pain relievers?"

SAAHI Todd rummaged in one of the drawers of his desk and drew out some papers and brochures. "You gals take these home and look 'em over. If you're still interested tomorrow, call for an appointment. And bring a checkbook." He stood, motioning for them to do likewise.

"But I have other questions," Petra said.

"Like what?"

"Like—like..." She couldn't think of anything to say. SAAHI Todd's brusque manner confused her. How did he ever get any students?

Jamie slid to the edge of her seat. "Here's the deal. Petra has juvenile rheumatoid arthritis. She needs to know if taking lessons would be good or bad for her."

Petra winced. She hated the name of her disease almost as much as the illness itself, and she didn't appreciate Jamie splashing it all over this strange man's dinky little office.

SAAHI Todd blinked down at Jamie, then at Petra. "Arthritis? Ain't you kinda young for that?"

"People get rheumatoid arthritis at any age," Jamie said, obviously enjoying her chance to seize the upper hand. "Too much exercise can cause flare-ups. How hard do students work out here?"

The man's droopy lid closed. "We have students with arthritis. They're all older than the two of youse. But you'll see when you read those testimonials how much our program has helped 'em."

Petra cleared her throat, unwilling to leave it to Jamie to explain her condition, especially as Jamie didn't believe she'd been healed. "I don't have it anymore," Petra assured the instructor. "I mean it's not active, but RA isn't anything like the arthritis old people get. It's really a problem with the immune system."

She paused, trying to think of a way to describe the disease. She could say that RA made a person's immune system so hyperactive it attacked his or her own body by mistaking something in the joints for invading microbes, but SAAHI Todd slapped the top of his desk before she had a chance.

"Just read them papers," he said. "I gotta teach a class." He waved his arms to shoo them out the beaded curtain.

Reluctantly, Petra got up. She had to say something else. Chas hadn't even been mentioned yet. "Uh, what's your name again?" she asked. "I mean your title?"

SAAHI Todd's eyes narrowed. "Why?"

"Oh, you know...for the check."

He reached over to his desk for a business card. "You can copy it right offa here. When you comin' back?"

"I'm not sure," Petra said. Then, because she couldn't think of any other way of working it into the conversation she blurted, "When does Chas LaGuardia come in?"

SAAHI Todd scowled. "You gals know Assistant Instructor Chas?"

Petra swallowed and glanced at Jamie, who shrugged as if to say, *Don't look at me. This was your idea.* "He goes to our school."

"Well, why didn't you say so in the first place? I'll have him answer your questions after you read over the material."

"You will?" Petra's pitch rose an octave.

"Call and make an appointment first." He opened the outside door for them. "And like I said, bring a check or money order.

Unless you got a credit card."

"Sheesh," Jamie exploded as they climbed into Petra's car. "Can you believe that guy? How can he teach martial arts? He looks like he sits around all day on his big fat ass." She puffed out her cheeks and made a round-belly gesture.

"Never mind him." Petra buckled her seatbelt. "Chas is going to answer our questions."

"*Your* questions, not ours. Uh-oh, speak of the devil...." Quickly, Jamie pulled the collar of her jacket up to her eyes and slithered down in her seat.

"What?" Petra looked outside. Chas had pulled into the parking space next to hers. For an instant she felt dizzy with joy. What better sign than this?

She watched him get out of a spotless classic Corvette painted shiny, metallic blue. He wore the plaid shirt and jeans she'd seen him in at lunchtime, but he carried a black gym bag with Master Lee's logo on it. Would he dress like SAAHI Todd for lessons, or would he put on sweats? Most likely martial arts clothes, Petra thought. Not that it mattered. Whatever his outfit, Chas would look great in it. Broad shoulders, narrow hips, muscular arms and legs.

"Is he gone yet?" Jamie crouched under the dashboard.

"He's going in the door now." Petra sighed. Why couldn't he have arrived a few minutes earlier? She started the engine and carefully checked her mirrors before backing away from the curb.

"What's taking you so long?"

"I don't want to bump Chas's car."

Jamie's head popped up. "But you're miles from his car!"

"So? You can never be too careful."

Jamie ran her fingers through her curly golden mop. "I wish you'd be *more* careful about this martial arts stuff. The main dude is rude."

"Who cares about him? We'll be working with Chas."

"We! What's this *we* business? I'm not coming back here."

"How do you know? You haven't read the testimonials yet."

Jamie barked out a short laugh. "If there's anything in that pile of crap that can change my mind, I'll—I'll…."

"Watch it," Petra cautioned. "You may have to eat those words."

"Ha," said Jamie.

Fighting a secret smile, Petra shifted into drive. It would suit her just fine to have Chas LaGuardia all to herself.

Chapter 4

Petra wanted to tackle the brochures and testimonials the instant she arrived home. She plunked her backpack on the creaky wooden porch swing and whisked a coffee-stained mug and overflowing ashtray off one of the arms in time to prevent them from crashing to the floorboards. When she opened the front door to set them inside, it was unlocked. Stale tobacco smoke lingered in the living room, providing further evidence that Alf Kroger, the latest in a long line of housecleaners, had breezed through.

Tugging the hood of her jacket over her head for warmth and breathing deeply of rain-scented air, Petra settled herself on the swing. From her perch she surveyed overgrown rhododendron and forsythia bushes sparkling with drops from this afternoon's shower. Time for her dad to announce a "lay weeder" party at church, she thought. Volunteers typically included the rectory property in their cleanup of church grounds. Petra fished a brochure from her pack. It looked like it might be the one Jamie mentioned receiving from Chas, *Work Hard: Master Lee's Philosophy of True Martial Arts.*

The first panel said Master Lee had established more than a hundred martial arts schools in the United States over the last thirty years. Each school was a franchise owned and operated by an individual who had been trained by Master Lee or by students of Master Lee. Petra laughed to herself. No wonder the great man wasn't at the Belville strip mall when she asked for him!

She flipped the page. Master Lee believed that Americans had grown soft and flabby, not only in their bodies but in their values. He aimed to right this wrong by introducing Westerners of all ages and walks of life to the Eastern secrets of long life and happiness through self-discipline and worthwhile endeavor.

"That's me," Petra said aloud, flexing her bicep and feeling its deplorable lack of firmness with her other hand. "Soft and flabby."

Wouldn't it be great to get back into shape again, to regain a sense of strength in her body? Petra stood and shot her fist at an imaginary opponent. Then she tried an experimental kick, noting small twinges in her joints from the unaccustomed activity. Nothing significant, though. Nothing that couldn't be overcome with hard work and determination. Master Lee's mottos. Petra executed another wannabe martial arts move—karate-chopping invisible boards—and caught a glimpse of her watch. Time to start dinner.

Inside the drafty old rectory, she hung her jacket in the entry closet and dug from her backpack the other material SAAHI Todd had given her. Brochures and testimonials she flung on the sofa before shutting the pack out of sight in the closet. As usual, Alf had left a pile of dirty dishes in the kitchen sink. She sighed and rolled up her sleeves. Half an hour later, Petra returned to her reading.

One brochure featured a cover photo of students in white pajamas lined up in rows like the people she'd seen in the park. In other photos men, women, and children tumbled on mats, punching or kicking the air—some alone, some in pairs. The blurb read, "Master Lee's School of True Martial Arts teaches a blend of tai chi, kung fu, tae kwon do, aikido, karate and judo. Master 'Springing Tiger' Lee studied the purest forms with the grand masters of Korea, China, and Japan. Nowhere else in the United States is such wisdom and artistry available in one school."

A price list was included. Petra gulped. She had nothing to compare it to, but the cost of lessons seemed terrifically steep. She had just begun to browse through the testimonials when she heard her father at the door. He whistled "Rule, Britannia." *Rule, Britannia! Britannia rule the waves. Britons never, never, never shall be slaves.* In Petra's experience, that meant he'd been preparing a difficult presentation to the vestry, a council elected by the parish to handle business matters, or that he'd had a run-in with one of them at the office.

Petra put down her papers and rose to greet him.

"Hello, my dear." He kissed her cheek and shrugged out of his raincoat, which had frayed at the collar and cuffs. Burberry, of course. Everything her father owned, and everything he did was so British. Peter Goodwyn had been London born and bred, educated at Oxford University, and ordained a priest in the Church of England before he immigrated to the United States after meeting Petra's mother.

Tall, silver-haired and dressed for work in black pants and shirt with a white clerical collar, Father Goodwyn stooped to peer at Petra over the top of his reading glasses. "You're looking unusually mysterious. Is there something I should know?"

"I have a surprise for you," she said. Petra had already planned how to get him in the mood for her martial arts pitch.

"Oh? A good one, I trust." He lifted his head and sniffed. "Is that it I smell now?"

"No, but it's a *Goodwyn*, all right. My special recipe for meatless lasagna."

"And that's not it I smell?" He sniffed again.

"I don't know what you smell. I haven't put anything in the oven yet—just got it ready and stuck it in the fridge."

"Oh. Last night's stew, then."

"Stew? What stew? I never make stew during Lent." Petra placed her hands on her hips. She wished her father wouldn't wear those old-fashioned half-glasses all the time. Sometimes people got the impression he disapproved of them when he gazed over the rims like that.

"Now I remember," said Peter. "Fish and chips, was it?"

"You know it was. You specifically requested that I stop at Ivar's on the way home, and you wanted *six* pieces of fish."

"Perhaps, then, I should take the contents of the dust bin outside. Whatever I smell is rather ripe."

"Oh, Dad!" Petra laughed. "Half a minute ago you thought it smelled delicious."

"My, my. How suggestible I am." He started whistling again and meandered off to his study.

Petra ran upstairs to change clothes. Although eager to get her father's okay to take lessons at Master Lee's, she knew it would be pointless to approach him before he had a chance to wind down. Besides, she enjoyed the leisurely time she spent with him—doubly precious because it could be interrupted or cut short by the demands of his profession. She liked their word-play, their friendly disagreements, and what she called his "Brit wit." She even liked managing this antiquated monster of a house on his behalf. It didn't get the care and attention it got when her mother was mistress, but Petra did the best she could.

Grandma Morse, her mother's mother, had been in charge for a while after her parents separated. Like Petra, Grandma suffered from rheumatoid arthritis and needed help with the housework. She had a knack for picking good people, though, which freed her up to drive her granddaughter back and forth to doctors and naturopathic physicians, making sure Petra followed their recommendations to the letter.

When Grandma moved to a retirement center last year, Petra's father had hired a succession of housecleaners to vacuum, mop, wash windows, and do the other heavy work. "You just can't find reliable domestics in this country," he remarked to Petra each time a cleaner gave notice. "I'll wager it has to do with your Constitution—all men, and let us not forget women—created equal," he'd say with an exasperated sigh.

Petra suspected the high turnover in housekeepers had more to do with their having to take orders from a young, apparently able-bodied girl. The most recently hired help had come from a small agency called Merry Moppettes. To Petra's astonishment, they sent Alf, a wheezy old man who spent more time on the porch swing smoking and drinking coffee than he did in the house. Petra said nothing to her father about Alf's work habits because he'd been nice to her and she didn't like starting over with new people. Besides, she'd hate to be the cause of the poor old man's dropping dead of a heart attack.

As she'd hoped, Petra's meatless lasagna hit the spot with her father. He ate three servings, claiming on the second and third he really shouldn't indulge himself, this being Lent and all, but his daughter's cooking had been irresistible. Petra suspected him of overdoing the praise, but she appreciated it anyway. Together they cleared the table and loaded the dishwasher. Petra was mentally rehearsing her entrée to the subject of martial arts when her father told her that the junior warden had called an impromptu vestry meeting for 7 P.M.

"Oh, no! You won't be long, will you?"

"Shouldn't be. One item on the agenda." He chuckled. "Pray that it doesn't multiply like the loaves and fishes."

Amen to that, she thought. "Will it be here or at the church?"

"We'll manage at the church. Wouldn't want our shouting matches to disturb your studies."

Father Peter wasn't joking. Petra had overheard many heated vestry arguments, sometimes about the silliest things, such as whether to put up storm windows in the nursery by November fifteenth or December first. "The precise timing matters to them," her father had said when she questioned him about that discussion. "It seems, on the one hand, that the babies like a bit of fresh air for as long as the season permits. On the other hand, there are heating bills to consider."

Petra closed the dishwasher and switched it on. She didn't offer to bake cookies from the frozen dough she kept on hand—no need to encourage anyone to get long-winded—but she did ask if he wanted her to make the coffee.

"That would be lovely, thanks," said Peter. "I want to jot down a few thoughts before I take on the enemy."

Petra knew her father meant the junior warden, with whom he had butted heads over more than one issue. His use of the word *enemy* was exaggerated, however. From Petra's perspective, what he felt toward the man seemed more like bewilderment than animosity. "I simply don't understand the fellow's reasoning," she'd heard him say repeatedly. "How he can add two and two again and again and come up with five is beyond me."

Petra brewed decaf, filled one large thermos with it and another with hot water. The vestry members could get cups and utensils plus sugar, creamer, and tea bags from the kitchen at church. Father Peter kissed her on the forehead and slipped back into his raincoat for the short walk across the rectory yard to St. Julian's. When Petra opened the door, a damp wind blew in, flapping Peter's coattails and making them both laugh. She shivered at the threshold until her dad disappeared into the darkness.

The papers from Sawhee Todd lay on the sofa, right where she'd left them. If her dad had seen them there between the time he got home and the time she called him to dinner, he'd said nothing. Petra felt lucky that neither of her parents intruded upon her privacy. They didn't pry, and they trusted her judgment. Well, and why not? She'd never given them any grief. Not like the kids she knew who got drunk and high or flunked out of classes. Not even like Jamie, who had her first sexual encounter in middle school. Petra wondered if she might be what her mother called "a good kid" because she wanted to please her parents, especially her father. Or did it have more to do with her illness, since she always had to be so careful?

"They give you the run of the place because you're mature for your age," Grandma Morse had told her once. "The same doesn't apply to your brother, though," she'd said with a shake of her head. "That boy would raise the hair on a frog."

Later Petra asked her mother about the comment, and Catherine had let out a loud guffaw. "Hair on a frog! Zeke's an active kid, barely eight years old. What does she expect?"

Zeke was eleven now, but Grandma's view of him hadn't changed much.

Thumbing through the martial arts testimonials, Petra saw that each displayed a photo of the author in a white-belted outfit. "No Pain, No Gain," ran the heading of the first. A middle-aged man wrote that he'd never experienced such happiness as when he felt the burn of a good workout at Master Lee's. "I know what

I'm doing is not only beneficial for me but for the world also," he said. "As Master Lee says, we earn our happiness. I am very, very happy to be earning my way in this community of the self-disciplined."

Petra had been taught that happiness was a byproduct of right relationships—with God, with others, and with oneself. But as she thought about it, she realized she had to work at those relationships, so in a way they *were* earned. She stuck the testimonial at the back of the pile.

The next one, although written by a teenager, proved to be a waste of time. Petra had nothing in common with the girl who'd been failing algebra until she entered Master Lee's school. "I didn't think I had a head for numbers," the girl wrote. "I didn't think I could do katas and other complicated forms, either. But the teachers at Master Lee's told me I could, and I practiced and practiced until I was doing them in my sleep. They told me if I studied that way, I could learn anything. They were right!"

She shuffled the papers until she found one with the word *arthritis* in the headline. The author, a thirty-two-year-old woman named Stacie, didn't say she had rheumatoid arthritis, but Petra thought she was too young for osteoarthritis, which her grandmother called "the other old-timer's disease," besides Alzheimer's. Stacie mentioned fatigue in her testimonial and spoke of days when she had to take handfuls of pain relievers to get through her work as a kindergarten teacher. All that had changed, she wrote, when she started practicing at one of Master Lee's schools.

Petra remembered the horrible exhaustion that had overtaken her before her last flare-up. And yet she had so much pain she couldn't rest. She couldn't even get out of bed without help. She too had taken fistfuls of over-the-counter medication. After several days of worsening inflammation and disability, her mother and grandmother had bathed her, dressed her in a long nightgown, and wrapped her in a blanket. Her father, weeping silently, had carried her to his car, and from the car to the hospital emergency room.

Logically, she couldn't imagine how Master Lee's program would wipe out the acute symptoms of rheumatoid arthritis, but she'd be more than willing to suspend disbelief to find out. Despite her declaration of healing, Petra still wasn't back to full physical capacity, and the hope that Master Lee could get her there was too powerful to dismiss.

Petra set aside Stacie's testimonial to show her father. Even Jamie should be impressed with the woman's experience. Petra reread the parts about how practicing movements especially chosen by her teachers had given Stacie boundless energy and erased her pain. "I am a happy woman," the article ended.

Closing her eyes and resting against the sofa cushions, Petra composed her own testimonial. *"Flash! Master Lee rocks totally and completely."* Better yet: *"Master Lee is kickin'! I have a life, thanks to him and his dedicated band of martial artists."*

She was sold, but her parents would have to be convinced. Petra just needed a little time to demonstrate Master Lee's ability to infuse her with health and happiness. And what could make her happier than saying goodbye to stiff joints, goodbye forever to measuring out her life in careful segments?

That's easy, Petra answered herself with a smile. Chas LaGuardia, of course.

Chapter 5

By the time her father returned from his meeting Petra had her new strategy in process. Twenty minutes before she expected him home, she assembled a baking pan, chopped walnuts, and refrigerated dough. Warm chocolate chip cookies and a tall glass of cold milk awaited Father Peter when he entered the front door.

"Ah," he exclaimed, his nose in the air. "You can't tell me that's leftover fish!" He took the empty thermoses to the kitchen and put away his coat. "You know the way to your old man's heart, don't you?" He joined Petra on the sofa, immediately stuffing a cookie into his mouth from a plate on the coffee table.

Petra pushed the plate at him. "Have two, they're small."

"What, only two?" He took another, but he bit this one in half and chased it down with a swallow of milk. "Excellent biscuits, my dear."

"Cookies," she said. "Biscuits are for breakfast."

"Very well, then. *Cookies*." He pronounced the word in a flat accent Petra knew was supposed to sound American but didn't.

"You do that on purpose, don't you? Say biscuits instead of cookies. Mother told me once that even in England they call chocolate chip cookies *cookies*, not biscuits."

"Do they, now? You have to remember I was born in the Dark Ages, before chocolate chips were invented."

"Oh, Daddy!" Petra made a hissing noise. "How was the meeting?"

"Unnecessary, in my opinion. But then my opinion is seldom shared by the junior warden." Peter yawned and stretched. "Finish your homework already?"

"Most of it. Plus I've been reading these." Petra waved the martial arts brochures and testimonials in front of him.

"Oh, yes." He took the sheaf of papers from her. "And what are they?"

"Well, Daddy, it's the weirdest thing. You know how I don't exercise and I'm going all soft?"

"Are you? I hadn't noticed."

"Just look at this." She invited him to feel her mushy bicep.

He pinched lightly with his long fingers. "Seems all right to me. What do you need muscles for? Isn't our friend Alf getting the jobs done around here?" He craned his neck to glance into the shadowed recesses of their high-ceiling living room, which Catherine had decorated in muted colors and a traditional style.

"It isn't that." Actually, she had been tidying up after Alf—there's only so much work a man can squeeze into a four-hour coffee break, after all—but that was beside the point. "It's just that I want to do things again."

"Do things, my dear?" Her father knit his salt-and-pepper brows. "What sort of things?"

"Martial arts things?" Petra pursed her lips, annoyed that she'd made it sound like a question.

"Martial arts things," he repeated thoughtfully, reaching for another cookie. "I must admit, I don't follow. Perhaps I'd better have a look at these papers."

"This one first." Petra pulled out the testimonial by the young arthritic woman named Stacie. Nervously, she snatched a cookie and munched as he read.

At last he looked up. "I'm afraid I still don't understand." He laid the testimonial on his lap and smoothed it like he would a table napkin.

"Jamie and I stopped there—at Master Lee's school—this afternoon. It totally made me think of St. Julian's. I smelled incense, and there were flowers and sayings on the wall. One was even from the Bible. 'All things are possible.' It's kind of a long story, but I feel like I'm supposed to take lessons there."

"Oh? Could you say a bit more about that?"

Yikes, her father had put on his pastoral counseling hat! Petra would need all her powers of persuasion to keep him from sinking her ship. She drew a deep breath. "Okay. Here's what happened. Jamie and I were eating lunch as usual, outside the cafeteria. We like to eat outdoors when it's not too cold or rainy. Anyway, along comes this guy. Jamie says his name is Chas and he's a student or a teacher, or maybe both, at this school, Master Lee's School of True Martial Arts."

Peter nodded his encouragement to go on.

"So we finish lunch and head in to class. I'm minding my own business, you know, just sitting there while Horseman lectures, and all of a sudden he says something about martial arts. Just out of the blue. And I think, wow, that's cool! Then we're driving home...." Petra stopped to reflect. "Oh, I forgot. First I meet Jamie in the band room to go over our assignment, and here she's doodled a cartoon of a guy doing martial arts."

She watched her father to see how he responded to her account. He'd quit eating cookies and was fiddling with the testimonial she'd given him, turning it around and end over end. Petra sipped some milk to clear her throat. Her father waited, methodically going through his routine again with the testimonial.

"After that," she said, "Jamie and I are in the car. I'm driving her home because she missed her bus. And *wham!* What should jump out in front of us, big as life, but Master Lee's School of True Martial Arts. It's right there on Thorson Avenue, on the way to Jamie's house. I never noticed it before."

"Hmm." Peter looked at her over the top of his glasses. "Am I to understand that you've drawn some sort of conclusion or made an interpretation regarding these things?"

"Well, yes." Petra had hoped it would be obvious.

"What, my dear?"

"Like I said, I think I'm meant to take lessons there. I've read all the brochures Sawhee Todd—uh, that's what I call him, the guy in charge of Master Lee's. He's got a supersized title I can't remember now. Seattle Associate...something. Anyway, the school teaches six different martial arts and one of them is this really slow, gentle thing called tai chi. You've seen it on TV. You know, those commercials for pain relievers? It looks like dancing under water."

"I know what tai chi is," said her father.

"Oh. Well, ever since I left Master Lee's I've been thinking about what you say in sermons, that God leads us through the circumstances and events of our lives."

"That sounds like a direct quote." He cracked a smile. "It's good to know that someone is listening to my sermons."

Petra sagged against the couch, suddenly aware of how tense she'd been. She felt certain now that she'd won him over. After a moment she added, "I also remember that you told us the Lord called Samuel three times, because often it takes three times just to get our attention."

Peter put the Stacie testimonial with the other papers. "Let me see if I have this straight. You believe, based on these—er—coincidences, that God is calling you to practice martial arts. Like God called Samuel to be a prophet in the Bible story."

She nodded, holding her breath.

Peter cocked his head. "But why, if I may ask?"

Petra pulled back involuntarily. She hadn't anticipated any *why* questions.

Why *would* God call her to martial arts? Because God wanted her to be happy? The brochures and the testimonials all emphasized happiness. And while she wasn't exactly unhappy now, she knew she'd be a lot happier with a boyfriend like Chas LaGuardia and a special kind of exercise to help her joints. Of course, no guarantee existed that Chas would ask her out if she studied martial arts. On the other hand, it was certain he wouldn't if he never met her in the first place.

"I think...." Petra began. "I wonder—Daddy, does God want us to be happy?"

Peter leaned against the cushions. "Excellent question," he said, staring off into the distance. "Jesus told a story once about a man who wouldn't think of giving his child a snake for dinner when he asked for fish. The father naturally wanted his child to have the best of everything. 'How much more,' Jesus said, 'will the heavenly Abba give to those who ask.'" He paused. "Yes, God wants our happiness. But Jesus taught that the oddest things make a person happy. You remember the Beatitudes? Blessed are the peacemakers, for example. *Blessed* means happy."

"Happy are the peacemakers." Petra liked it better that way. She tended to think of *blessed* as holy or saintly, which didn't appeal to her. At least not until she got older. Much older. Musing aloud, she tried to recall the other Beatitudes. "Blessed...that is, *happy*...are the merciful. Happy are the—what are the other *happys*?"

Peter stood and went to one of the bookshelves lining two walls of the living room. "Here, take this concordance." He handed it to her. "Look them up for yourself. You'll find some *happys* in Psalms and Proverbs, too."

She sighed. "Will they be under *blessed* or under *happy*?"

"Half the fun is discovery, don't you agree?"

Petra accepted the book and gathered up the materials SAAHI Todd had given her. She had no intention of doing anything with the concordance, but she didn't want to hurt her father's feelings. "Does this mean it's all right with you if I take tai chi lessons?"

"If you ring up your doctor first and do nothing more strenuous than tai chi, I expect it will be all right. But there is the matter of cost."

"I know. I have to talk to Mother about that."

"There's one other person I'd like you to speak to before you make any commitments."

Petra drew back. "Who?"

"It's not a requirement, just a request. Reverend Elisabeth."

"Oh," said Petra. "I guess that would be okay." Reverend Elisabeth was Peter's part-time associate. A twenty-something woman ordained to the diaconate last summer and to the priesthood in January, she had been called to St. Julian's to work with teens and young adults. Petra didn't know her well, because she rarely attended parish programs. Father Peter understood that a priest's daughter needs a life apart from the church.

"I'll just run these things to the kitchen, shall I?" Peter grabbed the empty cookie plate. "Rest well."

"Thanks, Daddy." Petra slowly climbed the stairs. Why did her father want her to see Reverend Elisabeth? Did he figure there might be more to the story than she'd revealed to him? Guilt pricked her conscience. There *was* more to the story, of course, but she doubted she'd be any more inclined to confess her crush to Elisabeth than to Peter.

She glanced at the grandfather clock on the landing. Why not call Mother now? She'd really like to get this martial arts thing settled. Tomorrow she could stop by the church after school. If she got lucky, she'd find Elisabeth in her office and be able to dispense with that obligation as well.

"Darling, what a wonderful surprise!" Catherine exclaimed when she recognized her daughter's voice.

"Am I calling too late?" Petra knew her mother was a night owl, but she'd learned not to plunge into any telephone conversation before inquiring about the other's readiness to talk. It was seriously deflating to be interrupted and put on hold.

"No, of course not. I was just going over the floor plans again for Hadley's Inn. My contact for that project is turning out to be a royal pain. Zeke's in the den with me, watching some mummy thing on television. It's almost over, and then he's going to bed. Would you like to say hi?"

"Sure."

Petra waited for her brother to come on the line. She could hear him complaining that his program had just gotten to the exciting part. "I'll TiVo it for you," her mother said. A few seconds followed during which she saw Zeke in her mind's eye, all freckles and spikes with a gap between his front teeth, glued to the set until Catherine could pause the machine.

"Hi," Zeke said into the receiver. His tone didn't convey much enthusiasm, but Petra remembered how forced conversations with relatives had bored her too when she was in fifth grade.

"How's it going?" she asked.

"Fine."

"What are you watching?"

"*The Mummy's Curse*."

"Is it good?"

"It's all right. I've seen it before."

"How's school?"

"Okay. I hit a homer at recess and slid in under the catcher's glove."

"Congratulations. Were you covered in mud?"

"I guess. I don't know."

"What position were you playing?"

"Batter."

Petra laughed. "No, I mean in the field."

"Oh. First base, like always."

"Awesome. I played shortstop when I was your age. I was pretty good at it, too."

Zeke didn't answer. Petra hoped he hadn't taken her words

as bragging instead of the wistful recollections they were. She couldn't know when she turned eleven that a few months later she'd contract a disease that would put an end to her involvement in team sports.

"Guess what," she said. "I'm going to study martial arts. That is, if I can get Mother to pay for it."

"Martial arts?" Zeke challenged in a scoffing tone.

"Yes, but not like the Jackie Chan movies. More like those commercials where it looks like people are waving their arms in slow motion."

Zeke snorted. "There's a big difference between Jackie Chan and the old geezers in those commercials. That stuff isn't *real* martial arts."

Petra bit back a sharp reply. "Maybe not, but I'll have fun anyway. Now let me speak to Mother again." Before he could set down the receiver, she called him back. "Wait, Zeke," she said. "I like you. Sometimes." Years ago Zeke had informed the family that *I love you* sounded icky to his ears, and that if they had to say it to "puh-leeze" use *like* instead.

"Me, too. I mean I like you, too. Sometimes. P.S., I bet Mom says no."

Catherine returned to the phone. "That was a one-sided conversation if ever I heard one," she said. "I hope you don't mind, darling."

"No, he's eleven. I get it. Uh, Mother, the reason I called is that I want to ask you something."

"Oh? What?"

"It's about taking lessons in tai chi."

"Tai chi! What brought that on?"

"Oh, just...things."

Petra could hardly invoke meaningful coincidences or signs from God with her mother. Catherine didn't share her former husband's faith, or any faith, as far as Petra knew. Petra had heard her say many times that during the years of their marriage she only tolerated religion "for Pete's sake," at which point she would laugh or smile or otherwise call attention to the double meaning of her words. If Petra said she believed she was meant to take martial arts, Catherine would probably roll her eyes and go, "Woo-woo," like she did whenever Dad mentioned prayer or guidance in her presence.

"What does your father say? Have you checked with your doctor?"

"Not yet. I'm sure it'll be fine, though. Daddy says it's all right with him, but you know he doesn't have the money to pay for it."

"And what makes you think I do?"

"I thought it wouldn't hurt to ask."

"Petra Cat Goodwyn, I'm already financing your car, your driver's insurance, and your cell phone. If I give you money for this, Zeke will be on me about that karate place again, and I don't have time to run him to one more thing. He's in scouts, and Tuesdays he has drum lessons. Thursdays it's soccer practice...."

"But soccer's not till fall," Petra protested. "Wait—what karate place?"

"Down on Thorson Avenue, at the end of the strip mall with that big black and white sign. Zeke's friend Jason has been taking lessons there, and every time we pass the place Zeke bugs me about it."

"Thorson Avenue? You don't mean Master Lee's School of

True Martial Arts?"

"That's it. How did you know?"

Petra almost dropped the phone. "Omigosh, Mother!" she shrieked. "That's where *I* want to take lessons!"

Chapter 6

The irony that Petra and Zeke were clamoring to take lessons from the same martial arts school apparently did not escape Catherine Morse's attention. She responded to Petra's announcement with a burst of laughter.

"Well, darling," she said, "I think you've just solved my problem."

"What problem?"

"Transportation. If you want to take classes at this Master Lee's school, I'll pay for them on one condition. You have to drive Zeke to lessons, too. I can't give one kid martial arts and not the other."

"Mother, that's so unfair! Zeke takes drum lessons and I don't."

"But you never wanted to take music lessons. You told us you hated piano, and you weren't interested in playing a band instrument, either."

"Drum lessons aren't music! They're just an excuse for Zeke to go crazy and make a lot of noise."

"Can you think of a better way for an energetic boy to work

off excess energy?"

"That's just it. Zeke's got his thing. Why can't I have mine? I don't want him messing up my—my...." Petra struggled for words. She didn't know what to call her new interest in martial arts. Her hobby? Her pastime? To tell the truth, she didn't want her chances with Chas messed up. How would she be free to hang out with him if she had to keep track of her little brother? Besides, he would embarrass her. He'd show off and hog the spotlight. Chas wouldn't even know she existed, except as Zeke's sister.

"I'm sorry, Petra. Those are my terms. You drive Zeke or I don't pay."

Petra sulked in silence, waiting for Catherine to back down or at least soften the blow. No such luck. The sound of her mother's determined breathing, undoubtedly through flared nostrils, told Petra that the world would quit spinning before she budged.

"I'll drop by tomorrow with the brochures and stuff," Petra muttered. "Sawhee Todd—that's the guy in charge at Master Lee's—said to bring a check or credit card."

"Sawhee Todd? What's that? Some sort of swami?"

"Yeah, I guess." Petra didn't feel like explaining the head instructor's title. She couldn't remember what the letters stood for, anyway.

"Tomorrow's impossible, sweetie. In fact, the whole week is shot with the Hadley project on deadline. I could manage Friday, though, if I work late on Saturday. Come about six-thirty. We'll do dinner at the Cosmopolitan."

Not till Friday? Petra chafed at the delay but couldn't afford to push the river. Her mother was a busy woman with a huge commitment to her work. No amount of pleading with her to pull back had ever succeeded in accomplishing anything but Petra's frustration. "Zeke, too?" she said, her voice edged with resentment.

"No, dear. Just us. Zeke will be staying overnight with Jason."

"Good. Uh, Mother?"

"Yes?"

"Would you find out if he really, really wants to take lessons at Master Lee's? I mean, you know how he starts things and quits two hours later. He's so into fads."

"I'll try, but don't get your hopes up. Earlier today I saw him standing in front of the full-length mirror in my bathroom, working himself into a lather, chopping the air and kicking his feet out sideways. I expect Jason has showed him some moves, or he gets them from his Wii. God knows, he spends enough time with that and all his other electronic games."

Petra sighed. Maybe God didn't want her to be happy after all.

* * *

The next day at lunch she sat on the bench outside the high school cafeteria, complaining to Jamie about what she considered a form of parental blackmail.

"Look on the bright side." Jamie nibbled a carrot stick. "Even if Master Lee's teaches all the martial arts at the same time, they wouldn't schedule children with older people. That'd be stupid, not to mention dangerous for the children. They probably even have more than one class for kids, because there's a big difference in size between, say, a four-year-old and a twelve-year-old."

"You're right!" Petra threw her arms around her friend.

"Why didn't I think of that? Maybe Zeke and I won't even have to be inside the school at the same time. Wouldn't that be great?"

"You're sure you want to go ahead with this?"

"Surer now than I was last night. Thanks, Jamie. You're brilliant."

Jamie grinned. "I'm just glad I won't be there. You couldn't pay me enough money to go back to that place."

"How come?"

"Ew, that Todd guy—the way he struts around like some kind of puffed-up peacock. Plus I'm bored with Chas. You will be too before long. He doesn't care about anything but martial arts."

"Shh!" Petra tossed her head toward the building across from them. Chas had just come out the door and waved at Jamie. Petra caught herself in time to keep from waving back. "Say something," she urged Jamie through tight lips.

"Hi," Jamie called. "What'd you think of that math homework?"

"Don't know. Haven't done it yet." He continued walking toward the cafeteria.

Petra elbowed Jamie. "Say something else."

Jamie frowned. "Hey, Chas, come here for a sec."

Suddenly light-headed, Petra patted her hair, brushed the crumbs from her sweater, and prayed she looked okay. Chas, of course, looked as hot as ever in slim-cut jeans and a sweat shirt with Master Lee's "Springing Tiger" logo on the front.

"Petra, this is Chas LaGuardia. Chas, Petra Goodwyn."

"Hi." Petra hoped she was smiling, not just baring her teeth.

Chas nodded at her.

"Petra's gonna take lessons at Master Lee's," Jamie said. "Maybe you'll be her teacher."

He spared a glance at Petra before turning back to Jamie. "What about you?"

Jamie shook her curls. "Uh-uh."

"Why not? You two could support each other."

"No way. It's not for me."

"Too bad." Chas shifted his backpack. "Nice to meet you—uh, Petra. Guess I'll be seeing you soon."

"Yeah," she said, sounding pathetic to her own ears. Other girls might say something witty, do something cute, but Petra couldn't think clearly, much less perform. Chas's disappointment that she, not Jamie, would be taking lessons was way too obvious.

Jamie nudged her after Chas disappeared into the cafeteria. "You okay?"

"I guess. I hope I don't freak like that during lessons."

"Don't worry. He did that to me too at first."

Petra thanked the powers that be for Jamie's adamant refusal to get involved with martial arts. She could compete with Zeke's attention-grabbing antics better than she could with Jamie's looks and personality.

"It doesn't matter, anyway," said Jamie. "You'll see for yourself that he's not worth stressing over. I give you…let's see…two weeks and you'll be begging to bail."

"Wanna bet?"

"You're on. A latte on me if you win."

Petra smirked. "Hot or cold?"

"What?"

"Say cold. I don't want to scald you."

"Ha-ha. In your dreams."

The rest of the afternoon, Petra struggled to keep her mind on high school. She imagined what it would be like to have Chas for a teacher, feel his touch when he corrected her positions, gaze into his brown-flecked amber eyes, and see him gazing back into hers. He might not know it yet, but she would make him forget he'd ever met Jamie. She would be the best martial arts student he'd ever taught.

* * *

Her father's battered Mini was not in the rectory garage when Petra drove in. He must be out on calls or visiting hospitalized parishioners, which meant that Reverend Elisabeth would be manning the church offices and Petra could get her promised consultation out of the way. Locking her books and things in the car, she shoved her keys in her jacket pocket and picked her way across the wet, sloping lawn to the church.

The young priest was on the phone, but she smiled and motioned Petra into her work space. A scattering of unmatched chairs and bookcases around an oversized desk littered with books and papers made the small, windowless room look more like a storage unit than an office—which it had been before Elisabeth's time. A fluorescent ceiling fixture cast a harsh glare over everything. Travel posters of Israel, Greece, Italy, Turkey, and Egypt had been tacked to the walls, most of them alarmingly crooked.

"Well, now," said Elisabeth after she replaced the receiver. "What brings you here?" She stood to shake hands. Petra noticed how plump she appeared in khaki slacks and a knit pullover. Up to now she'd only seen her in loose-fitting vestments. Elisabeth flipped back her long, ash-blond braid when she sat down again.

"Didn't my father tell you?"

"Tell me what? Please have a seat."

Petra pulled a chair away from the wall and sat facing Elisabeth. Nervously, she jingled the keys in her pocket. "He asked me to talk to you about—well, about some tai chi classes I want to take."

"Oh? Anything in particular about the classes?"

Petra shrugged. "It was my father's idea."

"Hmm. Well, he didn't say anything to me about it."

The two young women eyed each other across the desk, each at a loss for words. Elisabeth's phone rang.

Petra rose. "I'll let you get that. Sorry for wasting your time."

"No, no, you're fine." Elisabeth waved her back to her chair. "I'm going to let that go to voice mail. I've just thought of something. Maybe Peter suggested you talk to me because I earned a black belt in aikido before I went to seminary. It came in handy once in a subway station."

"Aikido?" Petra recognized the name of one of the martial arts taught at Master Lee's. "Is that anything like tai chi?"

"No, at least not in an obvious way. They're both about energy—that's what *chi* means in Chinese and *ki* in Japanese. Learning to use your body to focus energy. But for different purposes. Tai chi is solitary. You can practice it in groups, but it's a meditative kind of thing. Aikido is combative, a form of self-defense."

"And you used it on somebody in the subway?"

Elisabeth laughed. "Didn't have to, as it turns out. All I did was warn this guy who lurked around my bench that my hands and feet were lethal weapons. He gave me a half-crazed look, then vamoosed. I felt almost disappointed."

"You did?"

Elisabeth shrugged. "The newbie's curse—itching to use what you know. I've never had a chance to prove myself except on the mat."

"You mean in practice."

"Exactly."

"I wonder," said Petra. "Did you start out with tai chi?"

"No, I started with aikido." Elisabeth jumped up, her braid swinging out from her waist. "Would you like me to demonstrate a movement with you?"

Petra shrank against her chair. Evidently, Peter hadn't mentioned his daughter's rheumatoid arthritis. She didn't plan to mention it herself, if she could get away with it. "You mean here?" she stalled. "Now?"

Elisabeth glanced around her crowded office. "I see what you mean. How about out in the hall, where there's more room?"

"Uh," said Petra, beginning to panic. "Tell me what you're going to do first." An image of herself flat on her back with a broken arm popped into her head.

"Aikido is about catching your opponent off balance. With very little effort it's possible to flip someone to the ground. But it won't hurt, I promise. I'd like to show you how to throw *me*."

"Me throw you? With no training?"

Elisabeth dimpled. "Come on, you'll see." She opened the door.

Reluctantly, Petra got to her feet, her life flashing before her eyes. "Will there be any joint twisting?"

"Joint twisting? Maybe a little in the wrist. Does it matter?"

Petra looked away. When she couldn't think of anything else to do, she said, "I used to have rheumatoid arthritis. In middle school—not anymore—but I suppose I ought to be careful."

A flicker of dismay crossed Elisabeth's face. She returned to her seat behind the desk. "I'm sorry. I didn't know."

"It's all right. I asked my dad not to talk about it if he doesn't have to. I don't like people feeling sorry for me. Besides, I haven't had a flare-up in two years. In fact...." Petra swallowed. "I think God has healed me."

Reverend Elisabeth leaned across her desk, narrowing her gray eyes. "My sister has rheumatoid arthritis. She's had remissions that have lasted for years. Are you sure it's a healing and not a remission?"

Petra stiffened. "Does your sister have juvenile RA or adult RA?"

"Adult, but I'm under the impression that JRA is more serious, because the bones and joints are still growing."

"How serious it is depends on the person, not their age." Petra folded her arms over her chest. The last thing she wanted right now was a lecture on playing it safe. If she didn't take some risks, she'd never get anywhere in life. No pain, no gain, according to Master Lee.

"Look," said Elisabeth, pushing her chair away from her desk. "I didn't mean to be rude. Why don't you tell me about your illness, and about your—um—healing."

So Petra told her, surprised to find herself warming to the subject once she got into it. She hadn't realized how much she wanted an official verification that she'd seen the last of inflammation, fatigue, excruciating pain, missed school, hospitalizations, and the everlasting need to be cautious. Elisabeth listened closely, nodding from time to time.

"During my last hospitalization," Petra said, "I asked Daddy—I asked my father—to anoint me with oil and pray for my healing. From then on I got stronger every day. After I got home, on Sundays following Holy Communion, I'd stop at one of the prayer stations for more prayers. I must have had ten or fifteen different people praying for me. I know there's someplace in the Bible where it says if you pray and you have faith, you'll get what you ask for."

"If it's God's will," Elisabeth said.

"What do you mean?" Petra shot back. "Isn't it God's will for people to be well? And happy?"

The young priest smiled. "That's the sixty-four-million-dollar question, isn't it?" She looked past Petra to the door. "I believe God's will is a matter of discernment for each individual. Happy, unhappy. Well, unwell. Who's to say, because there are no easy answers or pat formulas that apply to everybody."

"You're saying that God might want you to be well and happy but not me? That's not fair!"

"I'm not saying that. At least not the way you put it. I'm saying that we all have to use discernment about God's will for us as individuals."

Petra frowned. She didn't like this maybe yes, maybe no business. Daddy's suggestion to consult a concordance was better than this.

"Take for example a decision you have to make," Elisabeth said. "Any decision. It could be the decision to pray about getting well. It could be the decision to accept your life as it is."

"A decision? What's healing got to do with—?"

"I'm trying to explain." Elisabeth thought for a moment, then snapped her fingers. "I've got it. Let's use your decision to take tai chi classes. How did you arrive at it? If we go through the steps of your process together, I'll point out the places where you had to make discernments—that is, judgments—about which direction to take."

Petra stared at Elisabeth, at the earnest gray eyes, the dimpled cheeks and chin, the wispy blond strands that had fallen out of her braid to frame her round face. If Petra didn't watch out, her father's associate would worm the whole story out of her.

Chas. Her crush. Everything.

Chapter 7

Two hours later Petra crossed the lawn separating the church and the rectory, her emotions in turmoil. Something about the way Reverend Elisabeth listened so attentively had prompted her to hold nothing back. Now she regretted it.

When Petra had finished pouring out her heart, the young priest asked questions. Unexpected, troubling questions such as, "Over the last couple of years have you experienced stiffness in the morning and evening or any other pain in your joints?"

Petra had downplayed the fact that she felt stiff most mornings and again at night, and that she sometimes experienced painful swelling in knees, shoulders, hands or feet that could last anywhere from a few hours to a few days. She'd grown accustomed to these discomforts and didn't think much about them. She didn't want Elisabeth to worry about them either. "It doesn't keep me from doing what I want to do," she insisted.

Elisabeth had nodded, but Petra got the distinct impression she disagreed, and it irritated her—as if Elisabeth knew more about her than she knew about herself. When the discussion shifted to Chas, Elisabeth had been even more bleak. She told Petra about being engaged to a young man who had cheated on her. "I used to have these gripe sessions with the Almighty," Elisabeth said, "about how James had been brought into my life—I thought by God—and about how important he'd become to me. I didn't think I could live without him. So why, I asked, did he go and break my heart? I found it very confusing, and it brought on a crisis of faith." She had hesitated before adding, "That was four years ago, and I'm still not completely over it."

While Petra appreciated Elisabeth's candor, she bristled at the suggestion that Chas would hurt her somehow. Politeness alone kept her from cutting things short by stalking out of the church.

Elisabeth seemed to sense Petra's agitation and lowered her voice to a soothing level. "I'm not saying Chas will be bad for you, or that martial arts—particularly tai chi—will hurt you," she said, sitting forward long enough to flip her braid off the back of her chair. "All I'm saying is that exploring such possibilities beforehand is a part of discerning God's will. In my experience, God speaks most clearly when we don't deliberately block out things we don't want to hear."

Petra recoiled. "What makes you think I would do that?"

"Nothing about you in particular. It's just that sometimes, when we—any of us—want something fiercely enough, we're willing to fool even ourselves in order to get it. I've certainly done my share of that." She gave Petra a hug as she left. "Please drop by again. I'll be praying for you."

At the house Petra saw her father's car parked next to hers. For once she wished he weren't home yet. She couldn't talk about the interview with Elisabeth until she'd sorted it out in her own mind and put the right spin on it. Elisabeth's pessimism might give him second thoughts about letting her take lessons at Master Lee's.

After retrieving her belongings from her car, she walked around the garage to the front door. Father Peter, dressed in his clericals, stood in the kitchen rummaging through the cupboards.

"Ah, there you are," he said. "Just back from church?"

"How did you know?"

He tapped his forehead. "Elementary, my dear daughter. When I saw your car with your things still inside and no Petra and no note in the rectory, I resisted the urge to indulge darker visions of kidnapping and arrived at the most logical conclusion." He chuckled. "In short, I nipped over there and saw you through Elisabeth's door. It was open a crack, you know, but you were both so engrossed you apparently didn't hear me."

"Oh." Petra changed the subject. "Don't worry about dinner, Daddy. I'll order you a pizza and salad from Mama Mia's. Did I tell you Mother and I are going to the Cosmopolitan tonight?"

"You did, and I hope you enjoy yourselves. I can manage my own pizza ordering, thanks."

"Okay, then." She turned to go.

"Aren't you going to tell me about your visit with Elisabeth?"

She tensed, her back to Peter. "Can we talk about it tomorrow?"

"Of course, my dear. You're not upset, are you?"

"No," she lied. "Just tired, and I have to get showered and dressed for dinner."

Petra climbed the stairs to her bedroom, no longer in the mood to go out. In the shower she debated postponing the get-together with Catherine but decided against it after trying a shampoo-in color rinse Catherine had bought for her. It smelled breezy, like outdoors in April, and it reminded her of how much she missed her mother.

Catherine came to the door of her townhouse condo looking trim in an ivory silk blouse and black side-slit skirt. Petra knew her mother ate sparingly and worked out five days a week at a health club to maintain her figure, which she showcased in designer outfits. She also knew the rich chestnut color of her hair came from a bottle, but that didn't take away from the pride she felt in Catherine's appearance.

"Darling, you look marvelous." Catherine squeezed Petra's hands. "What have you done with your hair? Is that a new dress?" She ushered her inside and helped her out of her coat. "Let me see you now."

Petra inhaled the spicy fragrance of Catherine's perfume as she whirled for her inspection. When she came back around, she glimpsed herself in the entry mirror. Not bad. She smoothed her dress, a shade of green that brought out the color of her eyes. She'd taken pains with her makeup, and her shoulder-length brown hair glinted with golden highlights. "I used that rinse you gave me. Like it?"

"Mm. Fabulous." Catherine kissed her. "My sweet little girl has grown into a lovely young woman."

Petra smiled. "You look wonderful, too, Mother."

"Thank you, sweetheart." Catherine returned Petra's coat and went into the closet for her own. "It's a shame to break up our mutual admiration society, but we'll be late for our reservation if we don't." She fluffed her hair and snatched a clutch purse off the entry table.

Petra glanced into the living room beyond. On the glass coffee table next to a vase of red tulips lay Zeke's handheld game player—the only evidence she could find that an eleven-year-old also lived here. Expensive modern furnishings in muted tones, lush tropical plants, and dramatic window treatments testified to Catherine's skill as a professional designer. Petra knew Zeke's bedroom would be another matter—a typical boy mess, in fact.

"Did you get a chance to talk to Zeke yet?" Petra asked.

"About what?'

"You know—martial arts."

"Oh, you mean whether it's a fad or not." Catherine opened the door. "Darling, he's ecstatic about the prospect of taking those lessons. I didn't have the heart. Now let's hurry before we have to wait in line like everyone else."

As Petra's last hope of having Chas all to herself faded, her spirits took a major nosedive. Catherine didn't appear to notice on the drive across the floating bridge to Seattle. Expertly weaving her Lexus in and out of congested freeway lanes, she kept the conversation alive with family news and work anecdotes. Petra tried to hold up her end, forcing laughs and commenting at the appropriate places, but her mind wandered from Zeke the spoiler to Chas the desirable and her two-hour meeting with Reverend Elisabeth. Should she share any of it with her mother?

When they were seated in a cozy corner of the restaurant, Catherine asked Petra if she wanted to celebrate their being together with a glass of champagne. Petra shook her head. She didn't care for the taste of alcohol, not even communion wine. She'd pretended to drink at the three or four parties Jamie dragged her to, but after a few sips she always got sick to her stomach. Possibly because of the way it mixed with her naturopathic supplements but more probably because she'd been repelled by the boozy guys she met who wanted to exchange bodily fluids before last names. Fortunately, Jamie didn't hold her social failures against her, although she did quit asking Petra to go with her.

"It's nice just to be with you," Petra told her mother, meaning it. She'd seen far too little of Catherine since the divorce. And Zeke didn't spend enough time with his dad, in her opinion. Like tonight. Zeke was at his friend Jason's when it would have been a good opportunity to do something with Peter.

"You seemed preoccupied on the drive over," said Catherine. "Is anything wrong?"

"Not exactly," Petra hedged. She had to speak louder than she liked over the Friday night crowd. She had been here on other occasions when soft music, the murmur of intimate conversation, and the tinkle of silver against crystal and china provided the backdrop.

The waiter arrived, and Catherine ordered white wine for herself, ginger ale for Petra. He handed them menus, recited a long list of specials they weren't interested in, and moved on to the next table.

"What do you mean, not exactly?" Catherine asked when they were alone again.

Petra weighed her options. She didn't want to infect her mother with any of Elisabeth's skepticism about her physical readiness to study martial arts, but she did want to vent her frustration. The more she thought about it, the angrier she felt about Elisabeth's gloom and doom. Her probing, pointed questions were clearly aimed at encouraging Petra to doubt her healing. Beyond that, she resented Elisabeth's comparing her jerk of a fiancée to Chas, even hypothetically. Chas was special. Different than the boys at Jamie's parties. Different than anyone she'd ever known.

Catherine leaned in. "You haven't changed your mind about Master Lee's, have you?"

"No, no. It's not that." Petra fixed her gaze on their table candle. All around them flames flickered in the semi-dark.

"Well, what is it, darling? Tell me before I burst with curiosity!"

Petra opened her mouth, closed it again. The waiter brought their drinks, and she had another few moments to think. Catherine probably wouldn't renege on her bargain of lessons for Petra so Zeke would have a ride. However, she needed to proceed delicately, because Catherine didn't appreciate God talk. Much of Petra's confusion about Reverend Elisabeth stemmed from the fact that they shared a belief in God's active involvement in people's lives. They just didn't come to the same conclusions, and that bothered her.

"For some reason Daddy wanted me to talk to his associate before I take tai chi," Petra said. "She has a black belt in aikido, which is a form of martial arts that's also taught at Master Lee's."

"Oh?" Catherine sipped her wine. "Sounds like they prepare the clergy to do more than love their enemies these days."

Petra laughed. Her mother's relaxed, down-to-earth attitude put her at ease. Even so, it took a while for her to spit everything out. She managed it with occasional anxious glances at Catherine to make sure she still had an audience. Whenever it looked like Catherine was about to make a sly remark, she toned down the religion. Once in trying to make a point Petra referred to the movie *Signs*, which they'd watched together on DVD, but Catherine pronounced the film "too far out" to take seriously.

"Let's cut to the chase," her mother said when Petra bogged down explaining the differences between how she and Elisabeth interpreted signs. "I think I see what you're getting at, but how did you feel about what she said?" Their food had come, and she picked at a chicken Caesar salad.

Petra took a bite of grilled salmon, barely tasting it. "Mad. Confused. I wished I hadn't gone."

"Why do you suppose your father sent you to her in the first place? What's her name again?"

"Elisabeth with an *S*. I've seen it in the Sunday bulletins, but I don't know much else about her—at least not until today." Petra put down her fork. "I haven't got a clue why Daddy sent me to her, unless it's because of the black belt. Her sister has RA, too. That could be part of it."

"Maybe he thought a woman's perspective…?" Catherine pushed her food aside, beckoned the waiter, and ordered another glass of wine.

Petra felt a twinge of anxiety. "Do you want me to drive back?"

"Darling, don't worry. I'll have a quart of coffee before we leave. You'll have some dessert. We'll talk. But if you're at all concerned, of course you can drive."

Settling against the padded booth, Petra said, "I think Daddy wanted me to hear Elisabeth's perspective as a priest. Someone other than my father. Like I said, she went on a lot about discerning God's will, as if she had the key to figuring it out. She tried to make me feel like I had jumped to conclusions about Chas, and like I couldn't do tai chi without keeling over or something. After a while, I got really pissed off. She acted like this all-knowing, all-wise 'authority.'" Petra put the words in finger quotes.

"That can certainly be annoying," her mother agreed. "Did any of her advice ring true to you?"

"No! Well, maybe. I mean...Mother, do you think it's wrong to go for a boy I just met? Not, like, stalking him or anything. Just making sure I get to know him better?"

Catherine laughed. "If there *is* something wrong with it, then half the world's male-female partnerships are in trouble."

"I wish you'd been there today to talk some sense into Elisabeth." Petra drew a breath. "I don't know why, but I felt from the moment I first saw Chas that I'm supposed to be with him. Not just *want* to. Meant to." She could feel the heat rising to her face and was thankful for the restaurant's dim lighting.

"I don't know anything about that," said Catherine. "I know even less about what you call 'discerning God's will.' I don't believe in a personal God, but I do believe in the forces of nature—in life and in love. It's what keeps us going, what makes us tick, what insures our survival. Sometimes you get hurt in love, but it's worth it, even if the experience is painful." She paused, holding her glass halfway to her lips.

"Did you ever believe—I mean like Daddy and I do?"

Catherine drank her wine. "No, I never did. I tried to, because I was oh, so head-over-heels in love with him. I went through all the rituals—baptism, confirmation, communion. I even learned to hold back from singing too loud, like a good Episcopalian." She flashed a wry smile. "I guess it didn't take with me."

"Is that what ruined it for you and Daddy? You couldn't share his faith? Maybe you couldn't respect his profession anymore?"

Catherine sighed. "Oh, sweetheart, it's more complicated than that."

Petra looked down at her plate. "I won't ask any more questions if you don't want me to."

"No, it's all right to ask. It's just hard to answer."

The waiter returned. Catherine urged Petra to get dessert, but she merely echoed Catherine's order for coffee. When it arrived, Catherine said, "Let me tell you about your father and me. I don't think you've heard the whole story of our courtship yet, and now may be as good a time as any."

Petra scooted closer to her mother, eager as always to learn more about the people her parents were before she knew them.

"Ready?" asked Catherine. At Petra's solemn nod, she began.

Catherine Morse had met Peter Goodwyn during an exchange term in London her junior year of university. Enchanted as she was with all things English, she'd sampled Anglican church services, including Evensong, a British institution more appreciated by visitors than by Brits themselves. Catherine had taken an immediate shine to the tall, distinguished-looking bachelor priest serving the parish nearest her flat. He presented an unusual challenge to her—a much older and different sort of man than she'd gone out with before. She'd set about gaining his attention by presenting herself as an inquirer into the Christian faith.

"Were you sincere?" asked Petra. "I mean about seeking faith?"

Catherine hesitated, swirling the ice in her water glass. "I thought so at the time. I didn't realize until much later that I'd acted on an infatuation, grasping at straws, doing anything I could to attract Peter."

"Why? What did you like about Daddy?"

"Oh, he seemed so wise. So self-contained. I thought he knew the secrets of the universe, or at least the secret of serenity. Maybe it was the uniform. Those flowing robes and stoles helped lend an air of authority." Catherine rolled her eyes. "Little did I know then that much of what I took to be wisdom and serenity was really absentmindedness."

"Now that's not fair," Petra objected. "Daddy is wise. And most of the time he's fairly serene." She thought for a minute. "Unless the vestry has just made him mad. Or he doesn't get his meals on time."

"Or any number of things," her mother said. "He's not a saint. And I don't mean to imply he's the opposite, either. It's just that I was madly in love, and he walked on water as far as I was concerned. Then."

Petra poked at her leftover vegetables. "What happened?"

"Time. Living together. Having children together. Realizing how much his religion meant to him, how little it means to me. More and more, we went our separate ways—him so ascetic and me the original material girl."

"Ascetic. You mean like a martyr or something?"

"Not a martyr, exactly. More like a person who doesn't really care about what kind of house he lives in, what kind of car he drives, or what kind of clothes he wears. Someone whose focus is on other things—invisible things. Like pleasing God, I suppose."

"Yeah, Daddy's like that. Except he does care about the food he eats."

Catherine smiled. "You know, I'd almost forgotten that, even as I've watched his waistline expand over the years." A wistful look crossed her face. "See how out of touch I am? Often it's the little things that destroy a marriage. Forgetting to notice the other person, forgetting to care. With your father and me, the small stuff niggled away at us until we both decided one day to let the charade go. We recognized we were no longer married in spirit, and hadn't been for a long time."

Petra was reminded of Elisabeth's dismal love story. "Did you—did you wind up hurting each other?"

"Yes, of course. It couldn't be helped. And I'm afraid we hurt you children, too. Don't you remember the arguments, the fights? We did what we could to keep them to ourselves, but I know they affected you." Catherine tilted her head at Petra. "I've often wondered if our fighting stressed you out so much that it brought on your last flare-up. Adolescence is such a vulnerable stage of life."

The waiter refilled their coffee cups. Petra added more cream to hers. She'd never considered the possibility that her parents' unhappiness could make her ill. Besides, that time seemed like ancient history now.

"I think Daddy needs you," she said. "He seems so lonely when he's not working. He never goes out unless it's something to do with church. He reads, or he listens to National Public Radio. I can't get him interested in games or movies or anything like that."

"He's solitary by nature," her mother responded. "You're like him—more so when you were little. You used to play alone a lot. But you're like me, too. A taste for adventure." She winked. "With any luck, you got the best of both of us, and not just our names."

"What? Oh, you mean Petra for Peter and Cat for Catherine. Mother, can I ask you something?"

"Of course, sweetie."

Petra chewed her lower lip. How could she put this? "Do you wish you hadn't married Dad? I mean," she rushed on, "if you had it to do all over again, would you still marry him?"

"If I were the same lovesick girl I was then, how could I help it? In a way, Peter was my destiny."

"Your destiny? You're saying fate brought you together, even though you ended up getting divorced?"

"More than that. I'm *glad* I married him—for two great reasons. I wouldn't trade you and Zeke for anything. But I'm glad I moved on as well. I'm enjoying my single state, relishing the huge variety of things life has to offer. Your father couldn't be bothered with the things I like. Concerts, theater, parties, travel. Destiny can take strange turns, you know."

"All this talk of destiny, Mother. Are you sure you're not religious?"

"No reason for religious people to usurp all the good vocabulary. Destiny is as apt a word as any to describe what's made me who I am."

Petra swallowed a lump in her throat. "You're not coming back to us, are you?"

Catherine reached for her hand and covered it with her own. "No, darling. What's done is done. Does that surprise you?"

"I guess not. You can't blame a girl for hoping, though."

"I don't blame you at all. I'm sorrier than I can say that things didn't work out between Peter and me, but it has nothing to do with how much I love you and Zeke."

"So," said Petra, glancing away to avoid tearing up. "You think it's okay for me to throw myself at Chas LaGuardia?"

Catherine's laughter pealed out. "Oh, baby, I can hardly imagine you throwing yourself at anyone. What I see is that you're attracted to a boy. That's natural. And you're tired of being cooped up. That's also natural. You want a change, you want to follow your heart, and I think you should. Wherever it leads."

Petra fell back against the booth and let the air whoosh out of her lungs. Her mother understood. "I think I'll have some dessert after all," she said with a smile.

"Good. They serve a mean cheesecake here." Catherine signaled the waiter. "And now, while I'm thinking of it, let me sign that check for you. The sawhorse or swami or whatever he is at Master Lee's can fill in the amount when you and Zeke register for classes."

Petra snorted. "You mean S-A-A-H-I Todd. The letters stand for Seattle Area Associate Head Instructor. I just say *sawhee* because it's shorter. He's something else. I'll have to tell you about him some time."

"Whenever you like, darling. I'm all ears."

Chapter 8

It took another half week before Petra and Zeke could start at Master Lee's. As Jamie had predicted, classes for children were separate from classes for teens and adults. "Score," Petra said under her breath when she found out the schedules over the phone. She signed Zeke up for Mondays, Wednesdays, and Fridays after school. She set herself up for Tuesday, Thursday, and Saturday lessons.

"Darling, are you sure you want to be committed six days a week?" her mother asked later.

"What choice do I have?" she said. "The only other option is to take classes at the same time as Zeke, and I hate the thought of it, even if they're in different parts of the practice room. You get it, don't you, Mother? I can't be worrying about him while I'm working on my own stuff." Besides, she thought, the more often I'm at Master Lee's, the more likely I am to run into Chas.

"Suit yourself, sweetie. I'm trusting you not to push your body to an unhealthy level, and I hope you find what you're looking for in tai chi." Catherine paused. "In your young man, too."

Contrary to his promise, SAAHI Todd did not let Chas

answer Petra's questions. Not that she had anything specific to ask at the time she stopped in after school to hand over her mother's check.

"He's teaching a class," the head instructor told her when she inquired as casually as she could when Chas would be available to go over a few things with her. "Take a gander through that window." He nodded to his right, where a door gave onto the practice room.

Petra got up to see. At the near end of the long mirrored room, a large African-American man with a thick neck and shaved head stood explaining something to a handful of adults in white outfits. At the far end, Chas led Zeke's friend Jason plus eight or ten other middle-grade children in an exercise that reminded her of riding a horse. He looked adorable the way he watched them so intently and patiently adjusted their postures.

"He does teach older people," Petra blurted out. "I mean...you said on the phone he'd be my teacher, right?"

SAAHI Todd motioned for her to sit down again. "You bringin' your kid brother in three days and yourself three days?" When she nodded, he said, "Assistant Instructor Chas trades off with Instructor Franklin—the big black guy you saw out there."

Petra cringed. She'd been taught not to identify people by the color of their skin, as if it were the most important thing about them.

SAAHI Todd continued, "Assistant Instructor Chas teaches the kids in the afternoon session Mondays, Wednesdays, and Fridays. He teaches new adults—that would be youse—on Tuesday and Thursday afternoons. It's hit and miss who you get on Saturdays. Could even be me."

"That's nice," Petra said, because SAAHI Todd clearly expected her to be pleased about his involvement. Not the greatest news, but she'd take her chances on Saturdays just to have Chas the other two days.

"It's better than *nice.*" SAAHI Todd's scarred eyelid drooped. "I'm a fourth-degree, which means I got advanced classes under my belt. It's a privilege to be taught by someone who's been personally trained by Master Lee."

"Uh-huh," said Petra, eager to be dismissed so she could watch the rest of Chas's class through the glass partition at the back of the practice room. Maybe even talk to him afterward.

But SAAHI Todd made her wait while he answered the phone and dragged out the paperwork—on purpose, Petra felt—probably mad that she didn't fall all over herself to kiss his feet. By the time she left his office, Chas and his young students had exited the practice room. She couldn't think of a believable excuse to hang around while they changed clothes, so she drove home fuming at SAAHI Todd.

* * *

The smell of incense mingled with humid sweat hit Petra like an exotic east wind as she pushed through the door of Master Lee's for the third time. Beyond the beaded curtain that led into the practice room, men and women punched right and left in unison, grunting with exertion while Instructor Franklin barked commands.

SAAHI Todd met them at the door. He directed Zeke to the changing room ("strip down to your tee shirt and jeans and take off them shoes") and told her to come into his office to talk about uniforms.

"What, now?" She glanced around in dismay.

He squinted at her. "Somethin' wrong with now?"

"No. I was just...I thought I'd watch...you know, make sure

Zeke gets started on his lesson okay."

"You leave his lesson to us. It don't start for another twenty minutes, anyway, and Assistant Instructor Chas is gonna have a little talk with him before he joins the class."

"Oh, like an orientation or something?" If Petra hadn't had to be home yesterday afternoon to pay Alf for his Merry Moppettes routine, she'd already be oriented and would have had her first class ahead of Zeke. Usually her father took care of the old man's compensation, but he'd been called away to deal with the death of an elderly parishioner.

Ignoring Petra's question, SAAHI Todd led the way into his cubicle and squeezed past two straight chairs to open the big metal cabinet in the corner. From it he pulled a white jacket on a hanger. A pair of wide-legged pants hung under the jacket. "This one's for you," he said before he whipped out another, smaller outfit. "This here's for your brother."

Petra's uniform looked enormous to her. "One size fits all?" she asked, wide-eyed. How could she look hot for Chas in a circus tent?

SAAHI Todd frowned and shook the smaller white suit at her. "This is a kid's uniform. It ain't the same size."

"I meant the other one. Don't you have anything in a seven?"

"You can shorten the pants or take 'em in or do whatever you gals do." He poked the huge uniform at her and laid the other one across his desk. Then he went around and reached into a drawer for two stiff, coiled things. He gestured to the only unoccupied floor space in the office. "Stand there and I'll show you how to tie your belt."

Petra shuffled to her right. "But I'm not wearing a belt."

"That's because I ain't showed ya yet." SAAHI Todd held out one of the coiled things, as pristine white as the uniforms.

"Oh." She made a grab for it.

"Not like that!" SAAHI Todd jerked away. Cradling the belt in his palms, he offered it again. "Take it with respect. Use both hands. It shows what you've earned."

Petra bit off a protest that she hadn't earned anything yet except a pain in the rear. She lifted the belt with exaggerated care.

"All right, now. Wrap it around your waist like this." He demonstrated with the other belt on the back of a chair. Quite disrespectfully, Petra thought. Why didn't he use his own belt and his own waist?

"It goes around twice or more," said SAAHI Todd, "and you knot it like so."

Petra tried to imitate his motions, but the belt got away from her and unwound to the floor, longer than a boa constrictor and twice as unmanageable. She stood holding one end of it and feeling like a complete fool.

"Never, never do that," he growled.

"I didn't do it on purpose." Petra retrieved the belt, yard by yard, looping it over her arm. She saw SAAHI Todd clench his jaw and sit down behind his desk, but she concentrated on the unwieldy length of stiffened material until she somehow got it wrapped around her middle.

"Take it home and practice," the head instructor said. "One more thing for now." He waited until she'd taken off the belt and tediously coiled it again. "You see these flags?" He shifted in his seat to indicate the flags on the wall behind him.

She nodded. "What's the one that's not American?"

"South Korea. That's where Master Lee comes from." He got up and bowed to the flags, bringing his right fist into his left palm as he ducked his head. "There's flags in this room and flags in the practice room, see? Whenever you enter or leave a room with flags, you bow. First to the flags, then to me, or whoever is the highest ranking instructor in the room, then to the next ranking instructor and so on. Last to the other students by rank."

Petra's mouth flew open. She'd never remember to do all that bowing! And how was she supposed to know the rank of an instructor or a student?

"Practice now," SAAHI Todd ordered.

Awkwardly, Petra executed a bow similar to the one she'd seen SAAHI Todd make.

"Not to me first," he said. "To the flags. And you're a beginner. You bow like this." He made two fists and dropped them to his sides. "You don't get to bring your hands together until you earn your black belt."

"But I feel stupid bowing to flags. I don't see the point."

"There ain't no point. You just do it."

Petra stared at him.

"Look," he said impatiently, "it's a sign of respect. You know what respect is?" Before she could answer, he added, "Wait a minute. Didn't you tell me your father used to be a priest?"

"He still is a priest," she said, unable to see what that had to do with anything.

"Still? Ain't he defrocked?"

"Defrocked! You mean kicked out of the priesthood? Why would you think that?"

"He got married, didn't he?" SAAHI Todd flashed a rare grin. "You and your brother are here, ain't youse?"

Petra regarded him with disbelief. "What are you talking about? We're Episcopalian, not Roman Catholic."

"Oh," said SAAHI Todd. "Episcopals have priests, too, huh? Well, I was raised a Catholic. We had to genuflect to the altar when we came into church and when we left."

"We do that, too. Some of us, anyway. Daddy's pretty high church."

"Okay, you got the idea. So bow."

Sucking up her pride, Petra managed a rigid little nod at the flags then at SAAHI Todd. "Can I go watch Zeke now?"

"Sure, sure." SAAHI Todd waved toward the beaded curtain. "Go see what you're in for."

Petra slung her purse over her right shoulder, draped the two uniforms across her left arm, and picked up her belt with both hands. Realizing that she couldn't take the other belt as well if she had to handle them both with the respect SAAHI Todd demanded, she said, "Is it all right if Zeke gets his own belt when he's done?"

"Yeah, that's okay. I need to teach him about the flags anyway."

"Thank you." She exited, parting the beads as quietly as possible.

"Hey, come back!"

Petra pivoted on her heel. Now what?

"You didn't bow."

"Yes, I did. You showed me the beginner's bow."

"That was practice. You didn't bow when you left the room."

"But my arms are full!" She thrust them out, loaded with uniforms, belt, and purse.

"That don't matter. Bow if you want to be a student at Master Lee's."

Petra froze, her gaze and SAAHI Todd's locked in wordless combat. If Chas was her destiny, then Todd must be her nemesis—a malignant force relentlessly throwing obstacles in the way of Petra's living happily ever after. She wanted to hurl her armload of uniforms at him and march right out the door.

Beads clattered behind her. She turned to look. Chas came into the hall from the practice room wearing the crisp white uniform she'd seen him in yesterday. Today she noted the black trim on his collar and cuffs plus a two-inch black stripe down the outside of each leg in addition to the black belt. Rank or no rank, tubby little SAAHI Todd couldn't hold an incense stick to Chas, Petra thought. He was so gorgeous, in fact, that he ought to be the poster boy for Master Lee's entire organization.

"Hi, Petra." Chas's expression softened, melting her insides. "Zeke's ready for that uniform now."

"What? Oh, sure." She moved toward him in a daze, hugging the uniforms to her chest. "You'd better take it out of my arms or I'll drop it."

Quickly, too quickly, Chas had it in his possession with just the faintest brush of his hands against her body. A spark of electricity ignited her skin, which burned feverishly in the afterglow of his touch.

"Zeke says you'll be starting tomorrow," said Chas.

"Uh-huh," she responded, all thought of defying SAAHI

Todd washed from her mind.

"Good. I'll see you then." He hesitated while she drank him in with her eyes. "Uh, are you finished in there?" Chas gestured toward the office. "I need a word with Seattle Area Associate Head Instructor Todd."

Trancelike, she murmured, "I'm finished."

"No, you ain't," SAAHI Todd called from inside.

"I mean," Petra said to Chas, "I'm almost finished." She spun on her heel and barely inclined her head toward the flags in SAAHI Todd's office. Lowering her gaze to avoid eye contact, she let go of her uniform and belt to make a silly stiff-armed bow to His Honor the Sawhorse.

A pickle-faced SAAHI Todd brought his fist to his palm in return, and she stepped aside for Chas. She lingered at the beaded curtain, taking her time picking up the things she'd dropped, catching a whiff of minty mouthwash when Chas bowed and requested permission to enter.

Well, she decided, if Chas can eat doo-doo, so can I. Just watch me!

Petra toted her stuff out to the car and tossed it in the back seat. She considered returning for the rest of Zeke's lesson, but if Chas was in with SAAHI Todd, somebody else must be teaching Zeke. She didn't care about anybody else. Tomorrow she would be in Chas's class herself. With any luck, she wouldn't have to do anything but grit her teeth and kow-tow in passing to the head instructor. She shuddered, wondering again how he kept any students. Wondering, too, how Chas could tolerate him, much less work for him.

"What'd you think?" she asked Zeke when he climbed into the car a half hour later, his new belt trailing in a mud puddle outside the door. What would SAAHI Todd do if he saw that?

Burst a blood vessel, probably.

Zeke reeled in the belt and scrubbed it off with his coat sleeve. "I like Instructor Franklin and Assistant Instructor Chas, but that Seattle Area Whatchamacallit guy sucks bad." He wrinkled his freckled nose. "Jason warned me about him, but I didn't think anybody could be that gay."

"Don't use *gay* like that," Petra said. "It's rude to gay people."

"No, it isn't."

"Yes, it is. Did Sawhee Todd make you bow to the flags and hold your belt like a precious baby?"

Zeke reddened to the roots of his spiky hair. "I bet Jackie Chan never did stupid stuff like that. I bet Jackie Chan could flatten that lard belly with one hand—one finger, even. I bet...." He twisted his neck and gazed out the window.

"What did you learn from Chas?"

"Assistant Instructor Chas—you gotta call him that. He'll make you."

Petra doubted it, but she didn't want to argue. "Okay. *Assistant Instructor Chas.* What did you learn from him?"

"Just simple stuff. Stuff I already know." He punched his fists, one-two, one-two, at the dashboard. "Can't wait till we start sparring."

Petra maneuvered out of the parking lot and merged with traffic. "Did he teach you as a group or individually?"

"Group. But first he talked to me in the changing room—told me all this crap about respect and waiting your turn. Like I was in kindergarten. Then he left and brought back my uniform, and I thought finally we're getting somewhere. But I still had to go to the fat dude's office to hear about tying my belt and bowing. I got maybe ten minutes in the class." Zeke stuck out his chest. "I didn't need any extra help, though. Assistant Instructor Chas told me I did real good for the first day."

"That's great," Petra said absently, trying to picture how it would work to have students at different levels in one class. Would everyone in her group be practicing the same thing? She had told SAAHI Todd she needed to stick to tai chi. Maybe she would be in a class by herself. Assistant Instructor Chas and his special student Petra. The thought brought a smile to her lips.

"Hey, watch it!"

Petra slammed on her brakes. She'd been tailgating. Now the other car signaled a turn. "Don't worry, I saw it," she fibbed. "Just testing your reflexes."

"Bull! You woulda crashed into his trunk if I hadn't hollered."

"All right, I'm sorry. I had my mind on something else. Thanks for saving us both from certain death."

Zeke grunted, crossed his arms, and slid down until he rested on his tailbone.

* * *

The message light blinked on the answering machine when Petra walked in the door of the rectory.

"Where've you been?" said Jamie's voice. "I dialed your cell a bazillion times. Call me."

Petra laid her uniform over the back of the sofa and respectfully placed the coiled belt beside it on a cushion. She opened her purse and saw that she had her cell turned off. Five messages and two texts, all from Jamie. "Call me as soon as you get this....You'll never believe what happened....Hurry....I need to talk....Drop everything....Now, not L8R...OMG, where r u?"

Fearing for her friend's life, Petra jabbed speed dial.

Jamie picked up in the middle of the first ring. "Jeez, Petra, where've you been?"

"At Master Lee's. Then I drove Zeke home. What's up?"

"Oh, yeah. Master Lee's. Well, it's about that, actually."

Petra's breath caught in her throat. "About Master Lee's? What do you mean?" In her mind the martial arts studio had burned to the ground and Chas was trying to pull SAAHI Todd out of the smoking ruins. Before he would allow himself to be rescued, though, Todd made Chas bow to the place where the flags used to be and then to him.

"I may be taking classes with you after all," said Jamie.

"*What?*" The smoking ruins of Master Lee's morphed into the ashes of Petra's love life. "You're not serious."

"Yes, I am."

"But why? What happened?"

"You know my petition to waive P.E. so I can take more art and music? It got bounced. My advisor told me during orchestra, and I sat in her office arguing about it till after the final bell. By then I'd missed you and my bus, so I started calling."

"But I thought your petition was okayed during winter break."

"It was. Now the school board's making the school take it back."

"They can't do that! It's the middle of the semester, and you're already enrolled in a bunch of required classes plus orchestra, chorus, and...."

"Drawing," Jamie supplied.

"Right, drawing. How do they expect you to fit P.E. into that schedule?"

Jamie heaved a sigh. "*They* don't care. They're assholes."

"But, Jamie—I don't understand."

"Simple. Before Christmas my advisor said no problem with the board, but new members were voted in last month, and they're back-to-basics freaks. *Voilà*, I'm SOL."

"There must be some mistake. I'm not taking P.E.," Petra pointed out. "Nobody said anything to me about going back on my waiver."

"You've got a medical excuse. Me, I have to take an extracurricular class in some physical activity, or I have to drop one of my electives. I can't drop drawing! It's my favorite class. I can't drop chorus! They need me for the spring concert. And I've played in band or orchestra since fifth grade."

Petra wanted to cry. "It's *so* not fair," she exploded. "Your advisor approved your waiver for this semester. That should count for something."

"*Should*, yeah. Doesn't, though. Believe me, Pet, I went over this looking for wiggle room like Nancy Drew with a magnifying glass. My advisor's gonna appeal for next year, but she can't do a damn thing about this one."

Overwhelmed, Petra stretched out on the couch. There had to be another option. Jamie couldn't take martial arts with her. Petra might as well paint herself invisible.

"Pet, are you there?"

Petra licked her dry lips. "What about the Belville Parks and Recreation Department? Don't they offer classes in dancing and aerobics and things like that?"

"Yeah. My advisor showed me a list, but they're all during school hours or after seven in the evening. So I decided to take tai chi with you instead. Hey, aren't you cool with it? I thought you'd be a little more enthusiastic."

"Um, well, I'm surprised is all. Last I heard, you weren't going near Master Lee's if your life depended on it."

Jamie laughed. "You warned me I might have to eat my words. Munch, munch. It just makes more sense to do it this way. I can take the classes immediately after school instead of in the evening when I'm busy with homework..."

Busy with boys.

"...and we can ride to Master Lee's together."

Petra sat up. Now was the time to play her trump card. "Jamie, did you check out their brochure? Very, *very* pricey. I wouldn't be able to afford it if it weren't for Mother." Jamie lived in a small apartment with her single mom, who worked as a waitress.

"Yeah, that bites, but I think I got it covered. When we were there last week I saw a help-wanted sign in the window of the Starbucks next door, so I went back to fill out an application. Interview's tomorrow during last period. Wish it was Horseman I'll be skipping, but *vive la France* and all that."

"*C'est la vie,*" Petra corrected. "That's what they say—means something like *that's life for you*—not *long live France*."

"Whatever. It's all Greek to me."

"French. Anyway, congratulations." Petra hoped Jamie couldn't hear the flatness in her voice. "I know you'll get the job." Jamie always got what she wanted.

"Thanks. Wish me luck."

"When do you plan to start lessons?"

"Depends. I'll talk to Todd after my interview tomorrow. Who knows? Maybe he'll give me a scholarship."

"I wouldn't count on it." Petra punched OFF, flopped back on the couch, and flung her arm over her face. Of all the martial arts joints in all the world, Jamie had to pick Chas's to be irresistibly cute in.

Forget about God not wanting Petra to be happy. God didn't even want her to have a decent day.

Chapter 9

When Petra arrived at Master Lee's the next day, her heart turning painful somersaults in her chest, she didn't know what to do. Chas's Vette wasn't in the lot, and she sure as heck didn't plan to consult Hizzoner Todd if she could help it. After waiting long enough to worry that Chas might not be coming in at all, she jammed her idling car into park and switched off the engine. A few minutes later, she climbed out, scanning what she could of the martial arts studio through the window, which wasn't much. The afternoon sun reflecting off the plate glass had her nearly blinded.

Sighing, she slung her purse over her shoulder and grabbed the carryall containing her uniform and precious belt. With her other hand she hefted her backpack. She'd been so afraid of arriving late that she'd come straight from school, edging over the speed limit the whole six miles.

Petra's legs wobbled as she walked to the door. Once inside, she stood inhaling incense and staring grimly at the framed message, NOTHING IS IMPOSSIBLE.

Wanna bet?

She checked her watch. Only a little earlier than she'd

arrived with Zeke yesterday, but the place was as dead as her hope of snagging Chas now that Jamie had decided to fish in her pond. It infuriated her. For Jamie, catching Chas would be child's play—just another conquest, another notch in her pole. Not for Petra. How could her best friend be so insensitive to her?

Shivering, Petra looked up and down the quiet, darkened hall. Was she expected to wait all day for SAAHI Todd to come out of his lair? Maybe it would be better to go back to her car until Chas drove in. She had her hand on the door when the head instructor stalked out of his office with a rattle of beads. She jumped. No matter what she did, Todd had a way of making her feel wrong about it.

"Where you goin'?" he demanded.

"To my car."

"Didn't we talk about bowing?"

"Yes, but I thought that was when I entered or left a room with flags."

SAAHI Todd exhaled noisily. "When you come into the school, the first thing you do is stop at my office. You stand outside the curtain, bow to the flags, then to me. That way I know you're here, and I can tell you what you need to know. Ya got that?"

"I think so."

"And any time you see an instructor, you bow."

"You mean like right now?"

"You're lookin' at an instructor, ain't ya?"

Once again, Petra was at a loss. How could she make fists and hold them rigidly at her sides when her arms were full? Jaw clenched, she bobbed her head at SAAHI Todd. The man defied belief. A Nazi in black pajamas.

"Work on your bow," he said. "Locker rooms are around the corner from the viewing area."

She crossed the hall and parted the beaded curtain to the practice room.

"Hold it!"

She whirled around. How could she have done something wrong already?

"Two things." SAAHI Todd held up two stubby fingers. "You bow when you leave me. And don't cut through there. Go around." He jerked his head toward the end of the hall. "I'll meet you in five minutes."

Petra's heart plunged. Meet SAAHI Todd? What about Chas?

Miraculously, at that moment the glass door opened and in he came, a stunning angel of mercy, bringing all the sunshine she needed with him.

"Hi, Chas." She beamed.

As if she hadn't greeted him, as if she weren't even there, Chas dropped his bag, turned to SAAHI Todd, and bowed.

The head instructor acknowledged the bow and squinted at Petra, his scarred lid twitching. "It's *Assistant Instructor Chas*," he told her. "Bow to me, then to him."

Petra flushed like a child who'd been scolded in public. Cheeks aflame, she went through the motions again with SAAHI Todd. When she bowed to Chas, she searched his face, uncertain how to act with him. To her delight, he gave her a look so welcoming it almost bowled her over.

"Hey, Petra," he said, his amber eyes twinkling. "Good to

see you again."

She floated down the hall in search of the women's room. Chas was worth every bit of humiliation SAAHI Todd could dish out. He alone made it possible to tolerate his boss, who reminded her of the psalm appointed for services last Sunday, one of the so-called "cursing" psalms. She had read beyond the part they'd done responsively in church to the place where the psalmist wants to smash the babies of his enemies against a rock. Never before had she appreciated the blood-thirsty passages of scripture. She had considered them barbaric. Now she understood. Only Petra would gladly spare SAAHI Todd's poor, innocent babies if he had any. She'd simply smash *him* to pieces.

When she found the women's "locker" room, surprisingly small and empty, Petra searched in vain for a locker. Two narrow benches ran along facing walls less than ten feet apart, the mirror on one wall and the door to the restroom on the other. She stowed her purse and carry-all under one of the benches and undressed in a hurry.

At first glimpse of herself in uniform, her breath rushed out like air from a punctured balloon. The waist had a drawstring, so she could adjust that, but the pant legs pooled at her feet, and the jacket sleeves hung well below her hands. Why hadn't she tried on the uniform at home? As if that would have made any difference. She didn't have a sewing machine. She didn't know how to hem things. When she or her father needed alterations, she took them to Grandma Morse.

Petra waded over to the full-length mirror, where she contemplated her reflection in despair. No two ways about it. She looked like one of those "after" pictures in which a newly svelte woman swims around in her fat pants to show how many inches she's lost. Maybe if she used her cuticle scissors to cut up the extra yard or two of her belt, she could tie her uniform at the wrists and ankles. Maybe she didn't need the pants at all—the jacket hit her at mid-thigh. That might catch Chas's attention.

The door opened, and four women crowded into the tiny room. One of them, a short, heavyset blonde about Catherine's age, gave Petra a broad smile. "I'll show you how to fix that droop, honey," she said, putting her purse and uniform down. She reached inside Petra's jacket and rolled the waistband of the trousers until Petra's ankles could be seen. Then she used the drawstring to secure it. "Roll up your jacket sleeves. I'll help you shorten them later."

"Thanks." Petra examined herself in the mirror. Not good, but better. "Are you a student here?"

"Yes, indeed. For the last month or so." The woman grabbed her uniform and began to change, bumping elbows with someone next to her. A flurry of motion and babbled conversation arose around them as the others shed their civvies. Raising her voice to be heard above the din, the woman said, "What's your name, honey? I'll introduce you."

"Petra Goodwyn," Petra shouted just as one of those weird silences suddenly fell over the group. While the others laughed, she grinned self-consciously. She couldn't remember anyone's name five seconds after she heard it until the roll call got around to the one who'd initiated it.

"Dee LaGuardia," she said.

"*LaGuardia?*" Petra cried. "Are you related to Chas LaGuardia?"

Dee chuckled. "You mean Assistant Instructor Chas? He's my son."

"But you don't look like him! I mean he doesn't look like you."

"I get that all the time. You know him?"

"Sort of. From school." It boggled Petra's brain to be standing in the half-naked presence of Chas's mother. Absolutely nothing about Dee's chubby, fair-haired, fair-skinned appearance or her extraverted manner reminded her of Chas. "What I mean is, we don't have any classes together or anything, but I've seen him around."

"Great! I hope you like it here. Chas talked me into doing all this grunting and sweating for weight control. I haven't lost a pound yet, but he tells me to keep at it." Mrs. LaGuardia shrugged. "Hang on and I'll show you how to enter the practice room. My guess is that Seattle Area Associate Head Instructor Todd hasn't said anything about it."

"He said I'm supposed to bow to the flags then to everybody according to their rank, but how do you know what anyone's rank is?"

"By their belts." Dee LaGuardia held up her own, which had a patch of black dyed on the white. "You earn your black belt in sections. I'm a first section. You'll get to know the students and their sections in no time. Besides, they're often all clumped together in the practice room and you just make one long bow to the whole group."

"Hunh," she said. "How many sections are there?"

"Six. The seventh is the black belt. The instructors are all black belts, of course. Seattle Area Associate Head Instructor Todd is fourth degree. He's the only one who wears black with white trim. Instructor Franklin is second degree. He has more black on his uniform than Chas, who just tested for first." Mrs. LaGuardia pointed one bare foot. "Take off your shoes, honey. It's tootsies *au naturel* around here."

"Okay." *Why didn't I think about a pedicure?*

While Petra unlaced her Reeboks, she got the second big shock of the day. Jamie burst into the room in her navy power suit and shopping-mall makeover face, her curls pinned up and lacquered in place.

"Jamie! What are you doing here? I thought you had an interview."

"I did. It's over. Todd said to go ahead and join your class, but I gotta pee first." She hesitated when she saw the door to the restroom closed. "Is someone in there?"

"Yes," Mrs. LaGuardia answered. "She'll only be a minute. I'm Dee LaGuardia."

"Hi. Jamie Francis. Are you any relation to Chas?"

"You know him, too? I'm his mother."

"Oh, cool. Jeez, Petra, you're swimming in that outfit."

You think?

Jamie ripped off her suit jacket and tossed it on a bench. "Good thing I wore the pants and not the skirt to my interview. Todd's plum out of uniforms till Saturday."

"What a shame." Petra kicked her shoes under a bench.

"Shall we wait for your friend?" Mrs. LaGuardia asked after Jamie scuttled into the restroom. "You seem kind of upset with her."

Petra looked away. "I guess. I'm not upset, just...I don't know." She couldn't explain it to herself, let alone to someone else. Fate, or a God who didn't like her very much, had apparently decreed that even her first lesson with Chas had to be overshadowed by Jamie.

Minutes later Mrs. LaGuardia led the two girls to a beaded curtain opposite the changing rooms. "Do as I do and you'll be all right," she advised, parting the beads and gliding into the practice room.

Petra watched her bow to the flags at the front and stand motionless until SAAHI Todd acknowledged her. She bowed to him, bowed to Instructor Franklin, then bowed to her son. Finally, still in the bowing position, she rotated her body to include all the students—adults and children alike—in one sweeping motion.

The spacious room's length was twice its width. A mirror covered the entire left wall. To her right Petra could see the door to SAAHI Todd's office and the beaded curtain which opened to the entry hall. She stepped inside, praying she'd remember to do everything in the proper order. Jamie came in after her and mimicked all her actions.

SAAHI Todd sauntered over to them. "I see the two of youse met Dee. You're with her over there." He indicated Chas's corner. "Take care of 'em for me, Dee."

She bowed. "Yes, Seattle Area Associate Head Instructor."

What? Petra's stomach churned. We're expected to say that mouthful and bow again every time the toad opens his trap? She didn't dare look at Jamie or they'd both lose their lunches.

As soon as they joined Chas's group, though, Petra felt herself relax. Every inch the professional, Chas gathered his charges and explained what they would be doing. He set the more advanced students, including Dee, to work on individual routines. Then he turned to the three new students—Petra, Jamie, and a skinny, acne-pocked man in his twenties who called himself Bruce Stir or Brewster, Petra couldn't be sure.

Chas showed them the opening movements of a tai chi sequence in which the students were told to step forward, draw their right hands from their sides, and thrust them straight ahead, then circle their left hands in front of their faces and push them out to the side. The final posture of that sequence reminded Petra of traffic cops she'd seen in old movies. Here we are, she thought, holding back cars and motioning little kids across the street. All we need are whistles to blow. But it was really fun. She enjoyed going over and over the movements, making them smoother each time.

By the end of the hour Petra had forgotten her anger at SAAHI Todd. She was elated, ready to take on the world. Assistant Instructor Chas—even his mother called him that during practice—had started her and Bruce (Brewster?) on the next movements of tai chi after he watched and corrected the more experienced students for a while. Petra could tell that her own motions were much more fluid than the man's, which pleased her immensely.

Jamie, on the other hand, had worked herself into a frenzy trying without success to do the first two movements. She lurched about like the Tin Man in need of oil. And Jamie—lovely Jamie—was soaked with perspiration. Even two coats of hairspray couldn't keep the frizz out of her face. Limp golden curls hung down her back, clung to her cheeks, and spiraled into her eyes. Mascara gummed her eyelashes, foundation streaked her cheeks. Her blouse stuck to her body with huge sweat rings under the arms. She scowled in frustration when Petra looked her way.

Chas rewarded Petra's performance with a special smile, the smile of a teacher for his highest achiever. "You did great, Petra. Really great. See you Saturday." To Jamie he said, "Don't worry. You'll get the hang of it eventually."

Jamie's scowl deepened. She stomped off, crashing through the beads to the changing room before Mrs. LaGuardia could offer comfort.

"I know how she feels," Dee confided to Petra. "This doesn't come easy for me, either. But you—you're a natural. Chas doesn't give many compliments, you know."

Petra thought she would burst with happiness. After watching Dee bow out, she followed suit, grinning blindly at everyone in the room. She even included SAAHI Todd in her radiant bliss and generously forgave him for frowning back at her like the sour old fart he was.

Chapter 10

Chas's approval had been reason enough for Petra to celebrate her first lesson in tai chi. But she had also experienced a physical high. Her body buzzed with awakened energy, and she couldn't wait to practice at home, maybe even outside when the weather cleared. She looked forward to learning more, studying the motions, putting her whole self at the disposal of this ancient and beautiful art form.

Jamie, who accepted Petra's offer of a ride home from Master Lee's because it had begun to rain, remained out of sorts. "How do you do that stuff? she said. "It's like slow torture." She kicked at the coiled white belt SAAHI Todd had handed her when they left and which she'd thrown on the floor of Petra's car.

"Why don't you put that belt in back?" Petra switched on her wipers. "You'll get it all dirty."

"Like I care." Jamie lifted the straggly hair off her neck and fanned herself. Her blouse was wringing wet. "Phew, I need a shower. And there you are, cool as an ice sculpture. You didn't even break a sweat, did you?"

"Sure I did, but it was fun."

"Fun, my *derrière*." Her friend stared out the window.

Hiding a smile she wasn't proud of, Petra changed the subject. "How'd your job interview go?"

"Fine. I think I nailed it, but they'll let me know for sure tomorrow." Jamie chewed on a blue-polished thumbnail. "Problem is I thought I would be taking classes at Master Lee's, and I gave the manager available work times based on that."

"So?"

"So screw it."

"Screw it?"

"You heard me. I'm done. Finished. Outta there."

Petra sneaked a sidelong peek to her right. While she had thought she would be relieved if Jamie quit martial arts, she felt disappointed instead. Clearly, her friend wouldn't be the competition she'd feared. Quite the opposite. Jamie was so clumsy, she made Petra shine in Chas's eyes.

"You mean you're bailing?" Petra asked. "Already?"

"Yes, already! Are you deaf or something?"

"I'm not deaf, but you're yelling."

"Only because you've landed us in some kind of cult. That moron Todd believes Master Lee is God and he—Todd—is his prophet. Stand by for the next Ten Commandments, the Gospel according to Struttin' Todd Peacock."

Petra decided to ignore Jamie's mix-and-match religious metaphors.

"Then there's Chas," Jamie raged on. "He goes around licking Todd's boots and acting like a dictator himself, while you stand there grinning like you're brain dead and eating it all up with a spoon."

"Brain dead! Spoon? What are you talking about? I didn't get you into anything. You got yourself into it. And Chas is not a dictator."

"Yeah, and Hitler was a saint. Ask anyone." Jamie slumped in her seat, arms crossed tightly over her chest.

"Come on, Jamie. You're being ridiculous."

"And you're being a PIA suckup. *'Yes, Assistant Instructor Chas. No, Assistant Instructor Chas. Your word is my command, O Exalted One.'*"

Petra glared at the road, trying to swallow her hurt and anger. She'd never known Jamie to act so insulting. The two girls had been each other's primary support system since Jamie transferred into Petra's school in fourth grade. If Jamie needed anything, a listening ear, help with story problems, Petra gave it without question. If Petra lacked confidence in her appearance or her social skills, Jamie told her she was too hard on herself. Petra expected Jamie to be happy for her now. Happy to see her doing well at tai chi when she'd been denied exercise for so long. Happy to see her making progress with Chas, whom she'd dismissed as boring anyway. What should Petra do—pretend that she was as bad at martial arts as Jamie?

"Hold it," said Jamie before Petra could put words to her feelings. "Forget I said that, okay? I'm a little pissed is all. It's just that I don't know where the hell I'm going to get the credits I need to fulfill that damn P.E. requirement."

A *little* pissed? "There's always the Parks and Rec," Petra reminded her when she could trust her voice not to quaver. "Also, you could check out extension classes at BCC and the U."

"I told you, they're all after six or seven in the evening."

"You didn't say anything about extension classes, only Parks and Rec. So what if they're after six or seven? I don't follow."

"Give it up."

"Just because you're unwilling to sacrifice your weeknight hookups—"

"Is that what you think?" Jamie jerked around in her seat.

"I don't know what to think," Petra said. "You tell me."

"All right. Listen up. Maybe you'll learn something." Jamie leaned in, her breath hot and moist on Petra's cheek. "Unlike you, princess, I don't have a rich mother. I earn my own way, and—guess what—it keeps me busy. School. Job. Homework. Sax practice—that's *sax*, not sex. Drawing practice. Spring concert. Drama Club. Cooking and cleaning and laundry because my mom works two jobs six days a week. Do I get a little time to sleep? Can I have a minute to go to the bathroom? God, Petra, welcome to the real world!"

Petra's face flamed. Maybe she had misjudged her friend, spoken out of turn, or come across as insensitive, but Jamie didn't have to be so mean. On impulse, she signaled her intention to move into the right-hand lane.

"What are you doing?" Jamie demanded.

Petra pulled into a Safeway parking lot and cut the engine. "Why are we fighting, Jamie? I'm your friend!"

"As if! That remark about me hooking up on weeknights wasn't exactly friendly."

"Okay, I'm sorry. I guess I didn't think about your other stuff—I mean saxophone and all that." Petra looked down at her hands, which were trembling on the steering wheel. "It just seemed like you were blaming me because Master Lee's isn't working out for you. Like I forced you to sign up or something. I didn't!"

"I know, but you're so into it. Can't you see the place is totally whacked?"

"It's a little weird," Petra agreed. She sat quietly for a few moments taking deep, calming breaths. The rain had slowed to a sprinkle, and the windows were steaming up. "I think the weirdness has something to do with Asian culture, though. We're not used to all that bowing. Probably even Sawhee Todd had problems with it when he was a lowly beginner."

"This is America," Jamie said. "We pledge allegiance. We don't bow."

"I get that. I don't like bowing either, especially to flags, but give it time, Jamie. It's only the first day."

"You wouldn't say that if you hated it as much as I do."

"What, bowing?"

"Bowing, scraping, sweating, stinking—the whole effing egg roll."

"You're right. I don't hate it—not the martial arts part. I love it. I feel like I've finally found something so...so perfect for me, I can hardly believe my good luck."

"Well, *la-de-da*." Jamie tossed her bedraggled curls.

If she'd slapped Petra's face, it couldn't have stung more. Petra wanted to *la-de-da* back, like she and Jamie were nine years old again, but she didn't dare. For whatever reason, Jamie was stewing in resentment, and Petra couldn't predict how she might react. She had no stomach for confrontation, so she fixed her gaze straight ahead through the foggy windshield and waited for an apology.

After several long minutes without a word from Jamie, Petra

flipped the key in the ignition and tore out of the supermarket lot. The rest of the way to Jamie's apartment passed in stony silence. Almost overnight the cherry trees lining the residential streets had burst into magnificent pink blossoms, but Petra barely noticed them. She drove up to Jamie's three-story, red-brick building nursing her wounds and rehearsing what she'd say if she could spew as easily as her so-called best friend.

Obviously unrepentant, Jamie yanked her purse and belt off the floor and climbed out, slamming the door behind her.

Petra jammed her car into gear, gunned the motor, and peeled away from the curb. At the corner, she rolled down her windows and blasted out a heavy metal radio station. The racket didn't take her mind off Jamie's rudeness, but it fit her mood.

* * *

"How did it go?" her father wanted to know as they sat down to dinner.

"It was...I don't know." Petra handed him a bowl of peas and carrots. "I really like tai chi, but Jamie isn't catching on. She acted like a jerk when I took her home."

"Maybe she's jealous," Peter observed.

"But she has everything," Petra fired back. "Well, almost everything. She made a big deal today about Mother's money, but that's not a reason to be jealous of me, is it?"

"Perhaps it is in her mind. You know, Shakespeare had something to say about this." Her father sipped from his water glass. "Beware the green-eyed monster. Envy, jealousy—they're not rational emotions."

"I know. I've always been jealous of Jamie's looks and personality. But that doesn't mean I don't want her to be happy! Why can't she be happy that I've found something I like to do, something I'm good at?"

"Hmm." Peter helped himself to a second scoop of potatoes. "I imagine she's not accustomed to being bested at things. It may take her a day or two to adjust to the new circumstances, but she'll get over it."

"You think so?"

"I hope so, my dear." He patted her hand and reached for the gravy.

* * *

Jamie didn't get over it. She got the job at Starbucks, which enabled her to continue at Master Lee's for the P.E. credit. It seemed to Petra, however, that she begrudged every minute spent doing martial arts. She also took offense at whatever Petra said about it. Yet they lunched together as usual, because Jamie had always made a point of shunning the cafeteria cliques and Petra didn't feel close to anybody else. Frequent awkward silences stretched between them, making conversation difficult.

After their third martial arts lesson, Petra had an inspiration. She had seen Jamie struggle unsuccessfully with the same few movements while she went on to complete several more sequences.

"Hey, Jamie," she said when they were alone in the changing room, "if you think it might help, we could practice in the school gym. I'm pretty sure it's empty at noon. I could—you know—watch and give feedback."

Jamie eyed her skeptically, but she didn't say no. The following day they ate lightly and hit the gym, Petra hopeful of a breakthrough. Less than ten minutes into practice, however, Jamie threw herself down on the bottom row of bleachers.

"I'll never get this," she shouted, her words echoing in the building's hollow expanse. "I'd rather have my teeth drilled!"

Petra had to concede that Jamie was incredibly uncoordinated and forgetful, but she suspected a mental block, like her friend's mental block with math. "Let's try again," she said. "We can go slower if you want."

"No way. It's a waste of time." Jamie stood up. "I'm going back outside."

"Well, all right, but I think you'd be fine if you could just relax. Go with the flow. It looks like you get mad at yourself, and that makes you freeze."

Jamie didn't answer. Petra trailed her to their bench wondering if another cold shoulder was in store.

Pale yellow daffodils and grape hyacinths had replaced crocuses in the flower beds. The air smelled of sun-warmed grass. Jamie whipped a book from her backpack, apparently signaling her wish to be left alone.

Two can play this game, thought Petra. She fished in her own backpack for her history text until a shadow fell across the bench. Looking up at Chas, she stammered out a startled "hi."

"Hey, Petra. Hey, Jamie."

Jamie kept her eyes on her book. "Greetings, Your Royal High Ass."

Petra saw Chas tense. She felt embarrassed for him and annoyed at Jamie, who in her opinion carried wounded pride to an extreme.

Chas shifted his attention to Petra. "How's it going?"

"Good."

"Looking forward to your next lesson?"

"Oh, yeah." She smiled, shading her eyes from the sun.

"You ever study martial arts before?"

"Uh-uh."

"You sure?"

"Pretty sure." Petra widened her smile.

"How about dance?"

She stared up at him.

"You know—ballet or tap? Jazz? Did you study dance when you were younger?"

"No. Never." Petra shifted uncomfortably, wishing for a quick infusion of Jamie's wit and charm.

As if summoned by Petra's need, Jamie jumped off the bench. "Please." She made a sweeping bow to Chas. "Don't let me get in the way of your masterful attempt to hit on someone just because she's with me. Have a seat, Romeo."

Horrified, Petra gasped, "Jamie!"

"*Excuse* me?" said Chas.

With a death look for each of them, Jamie hoisted her book bag and walked away.

Chas watched her out of sight. "What's with her?"

Petra spread her hands. "She's been like that since we started at Master Lee's. Attitude about everything connected with martial arts."

"Most students have a hard time at first," Chas said with a thoughtful nod. "I remember about a month of feeling like I wanted to quit seventeen times a day. Luckily, I had a good teacher."

"Not Seattle Area Associate Head Instructor Todd?"

"No. Head Instructor Juan. That was in Phoenix. I've only been here a few months."

"Right. Jamie told me—" Petra shut her mouth. Chas didn't need to know that she and Jamie had discussed him before they started lessons at Master Lee's.

"How'd you two become friends?" he asked.

"Fourth-grade seating assignments. Why?"

"Because you're so different."

Petra's gut wrenched. Here it came, the comparison with Jamie that would put her in the shade. "What do you mean?"

Chas peered at her with his brown-and-gold flecked eyes. "I mean you've got talent."

"I do?" Petra forced herself to hold his gaze, fighting shyness with every ounce of energy she could muster. She'd been called smart often enough but never talented. That had been Jamie's exclusive domain. Until now.

"Yep, you do." Chas glanced at his watch. "Can I walk you to class?"

"But I'm not going your way." Petra bit her tongue. Only a geek would say something like that. Her pulse pounded in her ears.

Chas laughed. "Then I'll go yours."

Thrilled, she zipped up her backpack. Chas helped her adjust the straps. In a daze she bumped along beside him to Horseman's class.

After taking her seat behind Jamie, who once again seemed to be absorbed in a book, she reviewed everything she'd said to

Chas on their short stroll. It wasn't much, but she must have done okay because he had smiled at the door. A nice smile, not phony or simply polite. She cherished the memory of him calling her talented, replaying it over and over until the period ended, when she realized that she didn't have a clue about Horseman's lecture or his assignment.

She tried to catch Jamie's eye as they packed up their stuff. "Um, Jamie?" she ventured.

"What?"

"Can I borrow your notes?"

"Why not? Go ahead and steal my work like you stole Chas LaGuardia." She snapped open her folder and thrust a sheet of paper at Petra.

Petra hesitated before taking the paper. "What do you mean, I *stole* Chas? I thought you gave up on him. I thought you couldn't stand him."

"I can't, and you're wasting your time if you ask me." Jamie headed for the door.

"Jamie," Petra said, "Why are you acting so weird? Have I done something wrong?"

"What do *you* think?" Jamie gestured to her notes. "You can give those back tomorrow." She strode out into the hall.

Like an animated cactus, Petra thought, with prickly arms that flail around and scratch people at will. She was so distracted by her friend's wigging out that for the next hour or two she almost forgot to daydream about Chas.

Chapter 11

After less than three weeks at Master Lee's, SAAHI Todd scheduled Petra to test for first section. Chas told her he'd also tested early, but not that early.

Her brother Zeke had been told he would test at four weeks, Jamie at six. Neither one seemed pleased with Petra's achievement, so she avoided mentioning it around them. Her moments with Chas became all the more special. Whenever they talked after lessons or between classes at Belville High, she sensed his admiration and gratefully received his encouragement. Hours of daily practice was a price she gladly paid to win his praise. She ignored the extra soreness in her knees, hips, and shoulders and tried not to mind the fact that Chas hadn't yet asked for her cell number, let alone a date.

The routine at Master Lee's generated a lifestyle so absorbing for Petra that in the middle of Holy Week, the week leading up to Easter, her father gently questioned her priorities. She usually attended the special church services between Palm Sunday and Easter. But her schedule at Master Lee's—three days for Zeke's lessons, during which she practiced, and three days for her own lessons, after which she practiced—left little room for other activities. Besides, she felt more tired than usual.

"Try to make Good Friday, at least," Peter urged her. "Our Lord watched and prayed for us. It's the least we can do for him."

It was so uncharacteristic of her father to nag that Petra didn't know what to say. "I'll try, Daddy," she answered, knowing she probably wouldn't.

The day Petra tested for first section, SAAHI Todd ordered her to his office afterward. Bowing and using titles had become second nature to her by then, so she didn't think he had any reason to find fault. Still, she feared that she'd slipped up somehow. Petra's mouth went dry as she followed the chunky little man across the practice room and down the hall. She waited uneasily outside the beads until SAAHI Todd beckoned her in.

"Take a seat." He pointed with his chin. "And gimme your belt."

"Excuse me?"

He snapped his fingers. "Your belt. You just made first section. Instructor Franklin has to dye it."

"Oh. Thank you, Seattle Area Associate Head Instructor." Petra untied her belt, carefully coiled it, and presented it to SAAHI Todd with both hands. He grabbed it and threw it in a drawer. So much for respect.

Shivering, she perched on the edge of a cold metal chair. She'd worked up a nervous sweat during the test, but she knew she'd done well—better than Bruce Stern, whose name she'd finally gotten straight sometime in the last week. Bruce messed up on that last sequence they'd learned, and SAAHI Todd had sent him to the changing room without indicating whether he passed or not.

"We need to get you into more movements," the head instructor told Petra.

She wasn't sure what he meant. "More tai chi movements?"

"A whole range of movements. Play your cards right and you could earn your black belt in a little over a year."

"My black belt? In tai chi?" Petra's pulse surged.

"Not in tai chi. In Master Lee's true martial arts. You need self-defense, *katas,* and other forms for that."

"Oh." Petra dropped her gaze. "I can't."

"Whaddaya mean, you can't?"

"I can't do things that would stress my joints."

"Nothin's gonna stress your joints." SAAHI Todd tapped his desk. "You let me do the worrying around here. Master Lee's forms release *chi,* bringing health and happiness. The more you put into your practice, the more you get out of it."

That sounded good. Petra had seen the advanced students practicing kicks and punches and complicated karate drills. She envied their skills. But she'd assured her doctor, her parents, and Jamie she wouldn't do anything more strenuous than tai chi. "I need to think about it," she said. "Can I get back to you?"

The head instructor's mouth curved down and his droopy left eyelid twitched. "You can go now."

Petra stood, bowed, and exited. It occurred to her that Master Lee might be a patient man, but his representative was not. If she didn't make up her mind soon, no doubt she'd find herself once again on the wrong side of SAAHI Todd.

Not that she'd hesitate if the decision were entirely up to her. Tai chi fascinated her, but the other forms attracted her as well. The desire to learn them all had lodged deep in her bones. But could she? Should she?

Dear God, send me a sign.

Petra thought about running over to Starbucks to talk to Jamie, who'd skipped the lesson today to work more hours. Not a good plan, she decided. Jamie's dissatisfaction with Master Lee's had settled to a dull roar, but she continued to question why anyone who didn't need to earn "abso-freaking-lutely stupid P.E. credits" would give SAAHI Todd the time of day. Beyond that, she'd probably accuse Petra of endangering her health. If only she could discuss it with Chas.

Petra dashed into the women's room, empty now, and changed into her street clothes. Then she fluffed her hair and freshened her makeup. If she hung around the viewing area, she could watch Chas until he left the practice room. After that, he'd be bound to pass her on his way out of the building.

But Chas wasn't in the practice area. Petra stood around for fifteen minutes in hopes of catching him coming out of the men's locker room. Fortunately, a couple of higher belts were practicing, so she had some excuse to be there observing them. When it became clear that Chas had already gone, Petra shouldered her backpack and trudged around the corner to SAAHI Todd's office. Chas stood at the curtain bowing out. Her heart leaped up like a trained dolphin.

"Hey, Petra." He grinned at her. "Congratulations!"

Petra didn't know if she should bow to him or not. Chas wasn't in uniform. To be on the safe side, she ducked her head.

He brought his hands together in the salute of a black belt. "You got time for a Coke?"

Petra couldn't believe her ears. "You mean now?" *Of course now, you idiot!* "I mean where?" *Shut up, you're ruining it!*

"How about next door?"

"Starbucks?"

"Is that okay?"

"Well, sure, I guess so." As long as Jamie didn't get bent out of shape. Petra paused at the door. Should she open it herself or wait for Chas to do it?

"Aren't you forgetting something?"

Petra whirled. Chas jerked his head toward the office.

"Oh, sorry." She went to the beads and waited for SAAHI Todd to look up from his paperwork. It took forever. He finally acknowledged her bow, his face impassive.

The next thing she knew, Chas held the door for her, then the door at Starbucks. Crowded with students and afternoon shoppers, the store's order line zigzagged across the entire entryway. Two baristas besides Jamie were busy behind the counter. Bob Dylan's plaintive wail rose above the rumble of voices and the whirring espresso machine.

Chas led Petra to a table that had just cleared and pulled out a chair. "What would you like to drink?"

"Drink?" Petra couldn't focus. Things were moving too fast. The music was too loud. "Uh, whatever. Anything's fine." She fell gratefully into the chair. Afraid of being spotted by Jamie, she plunked one elbow on the table, shielding her face from the counter.

"Cold or hot?"

"Huh?"

Chas raised his voice. "You want a cold drink or coffee?"

"Just ice water, I think. Thank you."

"Okay." Chas sounded disappointed.

"On second thought," she called after him, "I'd like an

Italian soda, please."

Chas stopped and turned. "What flavor?"

Flavor? Petra's mind went blank. She'd never ordered one before, only seen the name on the menu at Java Jive, where Jamie used to work. "Any flavor," she said after an excruciating pause. By then she felt ready to crawl under the latte-stained carpet.

Petra rested her chin in her hand. Through the screen of her fingers she watched Chas get in line behind a gray-haired man in a suit. She saw him strike up a conversation, sweep an arm toward Master Lee's, then reach into his jacket pocket for a brochure. The man accepted it, and they shook hands. Chas turned to talk to the woman behind him, who stepped backward shaking her head and trod on another woman's toes. Wow, thought Petra, how devoted is that? Chas must carry a stash of brochures everywhere he goes in hopes of persuading random people to check out the school.

Unsure how she felt about this, she scooted her chair around to view the counter. She could see Jamie, but she couldn't tell if Jamie had seen her. When Chas placed his order, Jamie's expression remained professionally pleasant. Same thing when she glanced out at the crowd and recognized Petra. No one would guess that she knew either one of them. Petra breathed a sigh of relief. These days she counted among her blessings any emo-free interaction with Jamie.

Chas returned, setting a drink in front of her. "They don't have Italian sodas, but they have sparkling water and raspberry flavor. Hope that's okay."

"Awesome. I love raspberry." She didn't, but who cared? She wouldn't taste it anyway. Her heart had begun to hammer so hard, she feared she might do something desperate. Like puke or faint.

Chas sat down and swigged his drink. It looked identical to what he'd gotten for Petra, only without the straw. "So," he said. "Congratulations again."

"Thank you." Petra managed a shaky smile. Why could she never think of anything to say? "I saw you handing out brochures."

Chas shrugged. "Part of my job."

Good. Not a fanatic, then.

He held up his glass. "Celebration time." It took Petra a moment to realize he wanted to clink their plastic glasses. As she lifted hers, he said, "Seattle Area Associate Head Instructor Todd told me you tested better in three weeks than most students do in six. He wants to add other forms to your lessons."

Petra set down her drink. "I know. I-I was hoping to be able to talk to you about it, actually." When Chas blinked at her with his luminous eyes, she felt unable to speak. Turning away, she mumbled, "I sort of promised my folks I'd stick to tai chi."

"You did? How come?"

"I had something—it made me sick when I was a kid. I'm sure I'm over it now, but you know parents." She produced a short laugh. Then she remembered that Chas's mother took classes at Master Lee's. "Oh, I don't mean *your* parents. I'm sure they're fine."

Chas looked puzzled. "What's wrong with your parents?"

"Nothing's wrong with my parents. Just—you know— parents in general."

"I'm not sure I understand." He cocked his head. "What did you want to talk to me about?"

Petra faltered. She stared at her glass, her mind racing while her tongue lagged behind a few million miles. The noise of the crowd and the music—Mariah Carey now—gave her a headache.

Chas cleared his throat. "Listen, Petra, I'm probably not supposed to tell you this, but Seattle Area Associate Head Instructor Todd is really impressed with you. He said he thinks you're instructor material."

"Instructor material?"

"He's been teaching for a lot of years. He knows dedication when he sees it."

"You mean...?" Petra swallowed. She couldn't bring herself to say what had entered her mind. Petra Cat Goodwyn, black belt instructor at Master Lee's School of True Martial Arts, working side by side with Chas LaGuardia, fellow black belt instructor. The idea was too sweet for words.

Chas nodded and sucked down the rest of his drink. "You're first section now. Back in Phoenix, Head Instructor Juan took me aside after I tested for fourth section and told me he wanted to groom me to teach. I wish—well, I wish I'd had time to complete my black belt before we moved—but that's not the point. The point is that Seattle Area Associate Head Instructor Todd will talk to you himself sooner or later. I just couldn't wait to let you know. Meanwhile, though, you have to do everything he says. You need to learn all the forms in order to teach them. And you have to trust him to know what's best for you."

Petra grabbed the edge of the table, suddenly lightheaded. How could she pass up a chance like this? On the other hand, could she afford to turn her health over to a martial arts school? She trusted Chas. SAAHI Todd was another matter.

"Hey, Petra." Chas grinned when she looked up, sending shivers down her spine. "You'd make a great teacher, you know?"

"Really? What makes you think so?"

"We need a female teacher at the school. The last one moved to Chicago before my time."

Petra drew back. It wasn't the answer she wanted to hear. "You mean Sawhee—uh—Seattle Area Associate Head Instructor Todd is only interested in me because he's got some kind of quota to meet? Like Affirmative Action or something?"

"No, no. Not like that. You're such a natural, he'd be interested in you anyway. But it's useful to have at least one female instructor in every martial arts studio so that the girls and women don't give up too soon."

"What do you mean?"

"Like inspires like. Take Jamie, for example. If it weren't for you, she'd have quit the first day."

Petra bit her lip. Hadn't Jamie told him why she signed up for lessons at Master Lee's? "I can't take credit for that," she said.

"I get it. You're modest, and that's fine. Master Lee expects to see modesty in lower belts."

"But—"

Chas laughed. "You're gonna love it, being a teacher. I promise."

Petra sank back against her chair, too flattered and intrigued to offer further protest. "What's the next step?"

Chas stood and put out his hand. "Let's go tell Seattle Area Associate Head Instructor Todd you're on for the advanced program."

Haltingly, Petra placed her hand in his. It felt warm and safe there.

Of course it did. This was the sign she'd prayed for.

Chapter 12

Petra put off speaking to her father about the new program at Master Lee's. He'd been on vacation after the demanding schedule of Holy Week, and she didn't want to stress him. Ditto with her mother, who had finished the Hadley project and committed herself to another deadline. Petra couldn't talk to Jamie either, so she kept her own counsel about eventually joining Chas as a martial arts instructor.

Twice she came close to blurting out the news, both times during lunch when an uncomfortable silence had descended between her and Jamie, but she stopped short, sensing that the less said about Chas and Master Lee's, the better. Since they were almost the only things on her mind, her contribution to their conversations was limited. Mostly, she listened to Jamie talk. Words, sentences, whole stories splashed over Petra like waves of sound, leaving few impressions and requiring nothing but an occasional *mm-hmm*.

Meanwhile, Zeke passed first section and was fifth-grade-boy obnoxious about Petra getting there ahead of him. "I had to know a lot more than tai chi," he said when he showed off his newly dyed belt. "Horse and punch, two kicks, and a chop—oh, and part of a *kata* drill, too. That's how come it took longer for me."

Petra clamped her mouth shut. It hurt to curb the thrill of being good at something with the people she loved. Sometimes she fantasized about being on stage—typically, the stage in the high school theater. From there she'd look out into the audience and see her father and mother, Jamie and Zeke, all her classmates and teachers, people she knew at church. Chas would come out from behind the curtain and together they'd demonstrate a complicated tai chi sequence to the astonishment of everyone. Petra Goodwyn, not just a math nerd anymore. But of course that was ridiculous. She didn't even like standing in front of a group.

As the month of April advanced, Jamie missed one tai chi lesson after another, claiming they needed her at Starbucks. The day before the scheduled test for first section, Petra offered to go over the moves with her in the gym.

"Save your strength." Jamie poked her mauve-tinted nails into an orange, jerking back as juice squirted out. "Todd told me I wouldn't pass anyway." She peeled the fruit, shook one hand over the grass, and licked her fingers.

"Why?"

"I don't practice enough, and I 'ain't got no respect.'"

"What'd he mean by that?"

"You don't know?" Jamie handed Petra an orange slice.

Petra ate it and wiped her fingers on a paper napkin. The real question wasn't what she knew but whether it would be wise to discuss it. "Well," she said as tactfully as she could, "I've noticed you don't bow, and you don't say, *Yes, Seattle Area Associate Head Instructor. No, Seattle Area Associate Head Instructor. Right away, Seattle Area Associate Head Instructor.*"

To Petra's relief, Jamie laughed. Then she dropped to her knees and bowed deeply to a rhododendron bush. "O great dickwad Todd," she intoned, "let me be your rug. Let me be your personal doormat. Let me fall prostrate at your feet."

Petra giggled, glancing around to see who else might be watching the show. Hordes of kids streamed by, but the few who paid any attention quickly turned away.

Jamie raised up, waving her arms, and bowed again. "May it please Your Lordship, Your Kahunaness, Your Totemic Grand Poobahship. Yes, sir. No, Sir. Thank you, sir." She scrambled off the grass with a swipe at the knees of her jeans. "See, I *can* be respectful if I want."

Petra smiled at her. How did Jamie get away with it? Not only the attitude but the spectacle. If Petra tried to pull a stunt like that in the middle of lunch hour, she'd be the laughingstock of Belville High.

"You think Todd would approve?" Jamie threw herself onto the bench, breathing hard. Red-gold curls haloed her pinkly cherubic face, prompting Petra to recall the old adage that appearances can be deceiving.

"No," said Petra, "but you obviously had fun. Maybe if you put that much effort into martial arts, you wouldn't be failing."

Jamie blew her off with a rude noise.

"What are you going to do if you don't pass?" Petra asked.

"Nothing."

"What do you mean, nothing?"

"I mean *de rien, nada,* zilch, zippo, nothing. *Comprenez-vous?*"

"Yes, I *comprenez-vous*. What I meant is how will you get

your P.E. credits? Doesn't the school board care if you attend lessons or not?"

"Probably, but I don't. I'm done anyway."

"Done? You're quitting for real this time?"

"Yep, only I'm not telling them, the clowns at Master Lee's. Let 'em figure it out for themselves."

"Is that...." Petra hesitated. "Is that fair?"

"Who gives a rat's ass? Those guys deserve what they get. You know Chas rags on me about lessons and practice every single day in math? How pathetic is that? I just look at him like he's from outer space. Which he is."

"No, he's not." Petra stared down at her clasped hands. The knuckles had turned white.

"Sorry. I forgot he's your boyfriend." Jamie crumpled her lunch bag and stuffed it into her backpack.

"He's not my boyfriend." *Yet, anyway.* "But I think he's nice."

"Well, you go on thinking that if it makes you happy. As for me, I don't care if I wind up dropping art *and* music. Don't even care if I have to do sit-ups or push-ups or laps around the football field every day and twice on Sunday from now till graduation. I'm never, ever taking another order from Todd 'thinks he's God'"—Jamie framed the words in air quotes—"Sweeney."

Petra twisted sideways. "Sweeney? Is that Sawhee Todd's last name?"

"Perfect, isn't it? Like the butcher who cuts people into mince pies in that Johnny Depp movie. Todd Sweeney, Sweeney Todd. Get it?"

"I get it, but how do you know?"

"Chas."

"Chas? Why'd he tell you? I mean, for what reason?"

Jamie arched an eyebrow. "Todd wasn't born with a fourteen-syllable title, you know. He puts his pants on one leg at a time, just like everybody else. Besides, Chas tells me lots of stuff. Some of it you don't want to hear."

Petra looked at her. "Like what?"

"Nothing. Forget it."

"Jamie! You can't say something like that and tell me to forget it. What wouldn't I want to hear?"

"Just about anything that might open your eyes to the kind of lame-ass voodoo they do at Master Lee's. Haven't you noticed how many people quit there? That guy—what's his name, Bruce something, who started with us? He bailed after the test you two took together. Todd wouldn't tell him if he passed or not, so he walked out." Jamie smirked. "He came in for an iced latte afterward, and we both saluted ol' Todd-wad through the wall with our middle fingers."

Petra hadn't known about Bruce, but she resented Jamie's implication that she made a habit of deceiving herself. Sure, some people started and stopped. They did in all sports. Why should Master Lee's be any different? The really dedicated people stayed on, worked hard, and got healthier and happier. That's all that counted.

Jamie continued, "Wake up and smell the coffee, Pet. Master Lee's House of Horrors, brought to you in living color by Sawhee Prick, is enough to creep anybody out. It's right up there with brainwashing centers and concentration camps. If you weren't crazy—and I do mean crazy—about that spaz Chas

LaGuardia, you'd have been outta there the first week."

Anger constricted Petra's throat. She'd had about all she could take of Jamie's insults. "How do you know what I would or wouldn't do?"

"I know you. I used to know you, anyway. I'm not sure who you are anymore."

"Well, that goes double for me. You've been mean and bitchy ever since we started at Master Lee's."

"Oh, yeah? At least I'm not a blind fool." Jamie bounced off the bench, slinging her half-open backpack over her shoulder. Her lunch bag fell out, but Petra wasn't about to pick it up for her.

She shivered. The sun, which caused her to take off her sweater when she and Jamie claimed their customary bench, had disappeared. A cold breeze sprang up. Black clouds threatened rain. Petra made no move to go indoors. She was stunned, dazed, unwilling to accept the fact that she and Jamie had come to this again. Ugly words. Hateful actions. Deep in her miserable thoughts, she didn't notice when someone veered off the sidewalk toward her.

"Hey, Petra, you look like you lost your best friend."

She glanced up. "Hi, Chas. It's not a joke. I really did."

He sat down, lowering his backpack beside him on the bench. With Petra's gear on the other side, the two of them were squished together in the middle. After a moment, he said, "So what's up?"

On an ordinary day Petra would be tongue-tied, but this wasn't an ordinary day. "Jamie—it's Jamie." Tears flooded her eyes. When Chas put his arms around her, she clung to him, sobbing out the history of her and Jamie's problems. "She—she thinks *I'm* the one who's changed," Petra cried. "I don't understand her at all."

Chas touched her wet cheek. "Looks like you need a Kleenex."

Petra straightened up. Self-conscious now, she rummaged in her purse for a tissue.

"Here." Chas held her sweater for her. "You're shaking."

"Thanks." She wriggled into it, dried her eyes, and blew her nose.

"So Jamie quit, huh?"

Petra nodded. "That's what she said."

"Maybe I can talk her out of it."

"I doubt it. She thinks you're an alien or something."

"An alien?"

"We're all nut jobs, according to her. Everyone at Master Lee's. Just because she sucks at martial arts. Plus she's not used to flirting with boys like you who don't pay attention to her." Petra turned away. Jamie would totally hate it if she knew she'd said anything like that to Chas.

Chas leaned back and stretched his arms along the top of the bench. "Master Lee's isn't about competition with other people. It's about doing the best you can for yourself. Maybe I should explain that to her."

"No." Petra swiveled around. "Don't you see? She won't listen to you. She won't listen to me. She just doesn't get it."

"Maybe. But I don't like to give up on anybody. Everyone needs Master Lee's."

Petra considered this. "Everyone?" she challenged.

"Yes, everyone."

"But that's impossible. People who hate martial arts? Sick people? Old people?"

A picture came to mind of her crippled grandmother pushing an aluminum walker into the practice room at Master Lee's. Next a bunch of her father's parishioners trooped through the beads, some in wheelchairs, others dragging oxygen tanks, all waving Korean flags. Alf Kroger literally swept in with the Goodwyn broom before curling up in a corner to smoke his Marlboros and drink his thermos of coffee. Petra had to cover her mouth to keep from laughing.

Chas didn't notice. He gazed across the commons, transfixed. A drop of rain hit his cheek, then his nose. Not a flinch. "Seattle Area Associate Head Instructor Todd believes that one day Master Lee's name will be a household word in this country," he said. "From here it'll spread to Canada, Europe, Australia, New Zealand, South America, even Africa." He slid around to look at her. "Just think, Petra. We're part of that. Part of a worldwide happening."

She gaped. She couldn't help it. The grandiosity of Chas's statement struck her speechless. Maybe she *had* gotten herself into a cult. The thought made her head spin. Hunching over, she put her elbows on her lap and hid her face in her hands.

Chas shifted beside her. "Come on, I'll walk you to class."

Numbly, Petra stood and hoisted her backpack. The last thing in the world she wanted to do right now was attend Horseman's lecture. She knew she wouldn't hear a word of it, and she thought it highly unlikely that Jamie would loan her any notes today. Petra needed time to think, time to clear her mind.

"Don't let Jamie get to you," Chas said. "It'll work out."

"You think so?"

"I wouldn't say it if I didn't." He steered her toward her class. "You up for a soda after your lesson? I want to go over your form with you."

"My form? What's wrong with it?"

"Whoa—nothing." Chas made the *safe* sign she recognized from softball. "It's fine. I've just got some tips—things I learned from Master Lee himself at a special session in Newark. That's where he started the first school, you know. Newark, New Jersey. It's where Seattle Area Associate Head Instructor Todd met him. If you want, I'll tell you how Master Lee saved our head instructor's life."

Petra opened her mouth to say she didn't give squat about how Master Lee saved SAAHI Todd, but Chas looked so pleased with his knowledge and so eager to share it, she couldn't bring herself to disappoint him.

"Okay," she said, thinking that when it came to martial arts, Chas acted like a wide-eyed little kid on Christmas morning. One-track mind to the max. Still, what right did she have to judge him? He might harbor a few strange ideas, but he was by far the cutest boy who'd ever shown any interest in her. Sweet, too, in his own way. Jamie had him all wrong. She just didn't know him like Petra did.

Chas said goodbye at Horseman's door.

After a moment, Petra called to him, her breath catching in her throat. "Chas?" She waited until he turned around. "Thanks. Thanks for everything. And would it be all right if we—you know—if we don't go to Starbucks?" She rolled her eyes toward the classroom to remind him about Jamie.

He transferred his pack from one shoulder to the other. "It's best not to avoid her, Petra. We have to keep chipping away at her resistance."

She grimaced. "Couldn't it wait another day?"

Chas backed down the hall with a wave and a smile. "Talk to you later."

Petra sighed. Not about Jamie, she hoped.

Chapter 13

That afternoon during practice, Petra's joints froze. Chas had been teaching her a kick that required her to pivot on one foot, then lift and swing the other leg straight out from her body. An amazing move. She'd admired Chas's execution of it and determined to do it properly herself. Her knees and hips simply wouldn't cooperate. Stabbing pain caused her to back off each time she attempted the rotation. Chas didn't criticize, but she knew she'd let him down.

After the lesson, she felt too whipped to protest his choice of Starbucks. Thankfully, the store wasn't busy. Soft jazz streamed from the sound system, soothing her jangled nerves. Petra sat at their table watching Chas speak to Jamie at the counter. She couldn't read his face. He turned and gestured. Jamie looked Petra's way, but when Petra fluttered her fingers in greeting, she didn't acknowledge it.

Chas set two raspberry sodas down on the table. Petra had never gotten around to telling him she didn't like raspberry. Gamely, she inserted her straw and sipped. "What were you and Jamie talking about?" she asked when he'd seated himself.

"I told her that you and I expected her to come back to

Master Lee's, where she belongs."

"You said that? *You and I?*"

"Sure."

"What did she say?"

"*No way.* Only she put it a little stronger than that." He pulled a face, and Petra imagined a few of the choice expressions Jamie might have used.

"Now do you believe me?" she said. "Lost cause."

"She may be lost, but she's not a lost cause." Chas swigged his soda. "I've seen others come back. Master Lee's is a way of life. Once you get into it, you miss it if you stop. And things don't go well for you anymore. You know what I mean?"

Petra did and she didn't. She adored martial arts. Everything about it—the way it looked, the way it felt, the sense of well-being it brought her in spite of increasing physical discomfort. But Jamie had never had a positive experience with it. She'd always been frustrated. Petra had gotten a taste of that today, trying to practice a complicated kick with irritated joints. She massaged her knees under the table.

Chas pushed his chair back. "What are you doing?"

She flushed. "Nothing. My legs are sore."

"Oh, well. No pain, no gain."

"I couldn't do my best today because my knees locked up."

"I noticed. I planned to show you one of Master Lee's techniques, but you were having trouble with the basics. Don't worry, though. It'll come."

"You don't understand." Petra needed to defend herself. She had a reputation to uphold.

"What don't I understand?"

She stared at her lap, where her fingers were busy shredding a napkin. Should she tell him about her rheumatoid arthritis? So far she'd only told Chas that she'd been ill as a child. She wanted to say more now. But if she did, it would be like admitting defeat, implying she wasn't well enough to earn a black belt and teach martial arts. Besides, maybe Chas had it right and her aching joints merely indicated progress in skill level.

She asked him, "Did your knees hurt when you first learned how to kick?"

"Sure. You get used to it, though. Especially when you know the hurt is good. It's leading to bigger and better things, and it's making you a stronger person."

"But I feel weaker when my joints lock up."

"That's just an illusion. Haven't you read the material Seattle Area Associate Head Instructor Todd gave you? Master Lee has a lot to say about how the practice of true martial arts builds strength, improves character, and promotes happiness."

Petra bristled. Chas didn't know her very well if he thought she'd neglect her martial arts homework—or any homework, for that matter. Of course she'd read the brochures and testimonials SAAHI Todd gave her. Several times. She thought of a retort, then realized Chas hadn't meant to slight her. He looked at her with such earnestness. A shaft of light from an overhead fixture illumined his olive skin, intensified the flecks in his amber eyes, highlighted his closely cropped dark hair.

Viewing him then, Petra glimpsed something vulnerable and unguarded at his core. She yearned to take his hand but felt confused about whether Master Lee's protocol between students and teachers applied outside the dojo. Under the circumstances, it seemed best to let Chas initiate personal things such as touching in the same way that he initiated what she practiced in martial arts.

"Could you...." She coughed to cover her uncertainty. Started over. "Could you tell me how Master Lee has made a difference in your life?"

"Of course. Be happy to." Chas settled into his chair.

Petra composed herself to listen, hopeful of learning more about Chas.

He told her he joined Master Lee's in Phoenix after his parents divorced. When his mother decided to relocate to Seattle so she could be near her sister, Chas had suggested the nearby city of Belville, where he could finish his black belt. "Seattle Area Associate Head Instructor Todd was great," Chas said, his eyes shining. "I hated to leave Head Instructor Juan in Phoenix. He'd been like—well, like a big brother to me. But Seattle Area Associate Head Instructor Todd made the transition as smooth as he could. He seemed to know just what I needed. You know what I mean?"

Petra's heart went out to him. How could it not? She knew only too well the hurt of a broken family. Although Chas hadn't expanded on the bare outline of what had happened, she could imagine how his favorite martial arts teachers might fill a post-divorce void in his life. "Do you miss him—your father?"

Chas glanced away. "Not really. I have Seattle Area Associate Head Instructor Todd and Instructor Franklin. And we all have Master Lee."

Petra didn't think even a hundred martial arts instructors could substitute for her own father. Maybe Chas had never had a decent relationship with his dad. Maybe it had been too painful for him to deal with their geographic separation. Maybe a lot of things Petra hadn't yet discovered.

"You mentioned that you met him—Master Lee," she said. "What's he like?"

"Like nobody I've ever known." Chas reached across the table for Petra's hand. A thrill shot up her arm to her brain, making her feel floaty. She had to catch herself from falling off the chair. "It's a privilege to be in his presence. You'll get to meet him, Petra. All the instructors do." Chas covered her slender fingers with his own sturdy ones.

Petra wondered if she should scoot around the table so that it would be more natural for Chas to hold her hand, but she was paralyzed with bliss.

"Master Lee—he's, well, a magic man," Chas said, tightening his grip. "No one moves like he does, not even in films. And his wisdom—jeez, it's off the charts."

Petra struggled to keep her mind on Chas's words, intensely aware of his hand, afraid he might take it away if she twitched her fingers. "Um…oh, wow," she stammered. "That must have been something."

"It was. And that reminds me." Chas withdrew his hand abruptly and leaned back in his chair. "I wanted to tell you about how Master Lee saved Seattle Area Associate Head Instructor Todd's life. Did you know that he—I mean Seattle Area Associate Head Instructor Todd—got involved with a gang when he was, like, twelve?"

Bereft of Chas's touch, Petra had to fake an interest in SAAHI Todd's misguided youth. "Really?" she said. "Only twelve?"

"Yeah, just a kid, but he was already into street drugs, knife fights, and petty theft. The older guys had guns, and once he got a flesh wound in a drive-by. Then for his initiation, Seattle Area Associate Head Instructor Todd had to beat up someone in the hood and rob him."

Good practice for his current job, Petra thought and immediately chided herself for being so negative. If SAAHI Todd had made that much of a change in his life, he deserved some respect for it. "So how'd Master Lee save his life?"

"That's the beauty of it," said Chas. "Master Lee had opened his first school on the turf claimed by Seattle Area Associate Head Instructor Todd's gang. One day Seattle Area Associate—"

"Excuse me." Petra lifted an index finger. "He wasn't Seattle Area Associate Head Instructor Todd then. Couldn't you just call him Todd?"

Chas frowned. "No, I couldn't."

"Why not?" Petra knew she'd made a tactical error by asking the question, but she wanted to know. Was SAAHI Todd SAAHI Todd everywhere, with everyone? In the bathroom shaving? In bed with his wife, if he had one? Back when he was a gangbanger?

"I just couldn't." Chas picked up his glass, sloshed the contents, and downed them in one gulp. He looked—not angry, Petra thought—but remote.

"Okay." She swallowed. "I'm sorry. I didn't mean to interrupt."

Chas shoved his sleeve back to see his watch. "I don't feed inside information to just anyone, you know." His gaze probed her. "I have Seattle Area Associate Head Instructor Todd's permission to share this with you."

Petra smiled to herself. So Chas didn't report things to Jamie he wouldn't tell Petra. Vice-versa, in fact. "Go on, please," she said. "I'd love to hear the whole story." She loved the idea of receiving special confidences, anyway. And the sound of Chas's voice, which was fortunate, because she heard a lot of it over the next half hour.

As if he had a personal investment, Chas poured out an elaborate account of SAAHI Todd's reclamation from the streets of Newark by his lord and savior, Master "Springing Tiger" Lee. Petra hoped she wouldn't be quizzed on the details, because they were blurry in her mind by the time the story, along with every grating repetition of *Seattle Area Associate Head Instructor Todd,* drew to a close.

"What about you, Chas?" she asked as soon as she felt safe to step off holy ground. "What do you do for fun?"

"Fun?" He stared at her.

"Yeah—fun. You know, outside of martial arts."

"Master Lee's is better than fun. Earning health and happiness is the most important thing in life. Teaching others the way is the second most important thing."

"Yeah, but you can't be doing that twenty-four, seven. You must have other interests."

Chas hesitated, put his hands on the table, then pushed to his feet. "I need to practice. I'm working on my second-degree black belt, and there's a test in a week."

"Wait," said Petra, panic bubbling up. "I mean, you're not upset, are you? You can tell me more about Master Lee if you'd rather."

"I'm not upset. What about Master Lee?"

"I mean—not about him, exactly. About...about you and Master Lee." She prayed her floundering didn't show. "About the school," she added. "You know, what you like about it and everything."

Chas sat down.

While he further regaled her with the glories of Master Lee's, Petra sneaked peeks at her watch. Forty-three minutes later he still rambled on. Not once in all that time had Chas grasped her hand again, or even acted as if it mattered who sat across from him. Yet she encouraged him with nods and questions, trying not to yawn or think about how stiff her joints were. The murmur of surrounding conversation, rising and falling to the tunes of Kenny G, made her sleepy. She traced words on the tabletop to keep her eyes open. *Chas. LaGuardia. Quit. Talking. Now.*

It wouldn't have been so bad if he'd stuck to his own experience instead of reverting to Master Lee's philosophy. *Work hard. Obey higher belts. Act healthy, be healthy. Pass it on.* Petra had heard it all before, and she'd definitely lost her appetite for it. If Chas couldn't talk about anything else, she'd be better off alone. On the other hand, maybe he just needed to get all this stuff out of his system—make sure she was on the same page with him—before he could move on.

"Thanks, Chas," Petra said when he appeared to be winding down. "You've been very helpful. I'll remember what you said about 'no pain, no gain,' too."

"Good." He stood and stretched. "I'm glad we talked. It's important for you to understand about Master Lee. You may be a teacher yourself some day."

May be. Petra didn't like the sound of that. Had he taken a step back from her just because she asked what he did for fun?

Chas collected their soda containers and napkins. Petra's glass was more than half full of syrupy muck and melted ice. He held it up. "Something wrong with this?"

"It's...well, maybe next time I could try another flavor."

Petra swallowed hard. What had she done? Acted ungrateful and, as if that wasn't bad enough, assumed there would be a next time.

Chas didn't respond. She couldn't tell what he thought or felt as he walked their trash to the wastebasket and jammed it inside. He waited for her at the door, and they exited Starbucks in silence.

"See you, Petra," he said, thumping the hood of her car.

She nodded and dug in her purse for her keys. By the time she retrieved them, Chas had climbed into his shiny blue Corvette. Why did he tell her he needed to work on his upcoming test at Master Lee's if he had no intention of doing so? Had she kept him too long? Where would he go now?

It bothered her to know so little about Chas after all the hours they'd spent together. She watched him back up and drive away. Sighing, she checked the time, saw that it was late, and remembered that her father had been invited to dinner with the ministerial association.

Petra lingered for a moment outside Master Lee's regarding the life-sized cutout of a young "Springing Tiger" in action before she reached into the back seat of her car. Damp and disgusting as her uniform was sure to be, she knew SAAHI Todd wouldn't let her practice without it.

And practice she must if she wanted to be good enough for Chas.

Chapter 14

In the weeks that followed, Petra practiced harder and longer, ignoring the pain in her joints. Some days her knees or hips would seize up and she had to quit, knowing that Chas thought she'd wimped out. Often she dragged through the afternoon and fell into bed after dinner. Her father commented on her fatigue, but she insisted she'd never felt better in her life. Master Lee's "think healthy, be healthy" advice rang in her ears. Once in a while Chas treated her to a soda—chocolate at her request—but it was all she could do to keep from nodding off while he dispensed Master Lee's words of wisdom.

Early in May, a guidance counselor invited Petra into her office to talk about her academic future. A program called Running Start would enable her to finish her last two years of high school at Belville Community College. If she chose to take the opportunity, offered to a select number of gifted students, she would graduate from college two years ahead of her peers, and part of it would be paid for by the State of Washington.

Petra promised to discuss the possibility with her parents, but she had doubts about the program. College might interfere with her schedule at Master Lee's. She'd passed second section by then and was scheduled to test for third in a few days. The number of hours she needed to spend in practice had multiplied as she advanced in rank. Besides, if she did Running Start, she'd be leaving Chas and Jamie behind.

She and Jamie weren't as close as they used to be, but for Petra any level of friendship was better than none. After their last rift, they'd gradually resumed their customary sharing of lunches, notes, and gossip. Everything but the easy give-and-take they once enjoyed. Petra stayed on guard now lest she accidentally disrupt their fragile truce. As for Jamie, she didn't go back to Master Lee's or earn P.E. credits anywhere else. With the help of her advisor, she'd filed an appeal with the district, claiming that the new school board's demands presented an unreasonable hardship.

At lunch one day, Petra mentioned Running Start. "I guess I should be excited," she said, "but I'm not. What would you do?"

Jamie looked at her. "Seriously? Out of high school this year, out of college by twenty? That's a no-brainer."

"But wouldn't you miss me if it were you?"

Jamie took a banana out of her lunch bag, peeled part of it, and broke off a piece for Petra. "We'd still be friends."

Petra wasn't so sure of that. She ate the banana but let the peanut butter and cheese crackers she'd packed for herself drop into her lap unopened.

Jamie swung around to her. "Wait a minute. You didn't say no, did you?"

Petra shook her head. "I said I wanted to think about it." She'd been so sure Jamie would encourage her to stay at Belville High, she hardly knew what to do without her support.

"I don't get it," said Jamie. "What's to think?"

Petra picked at the plastic wrap over her crackers. Her head ached.

Jamie asked, "Have you talked to your boyfriend about this yet?" When Petra frowned, she added, "I mean Chas the spaz."

"I know who you mean, and he's not a spaz. You should see him do martial arts."

"I have seen him. It's an insult, not a description."

"But why do you have to insult him in the first place?"

"Because the guy's the dimmest bulb I ever met. Did you know that all the while he's waiting for an order at Starbucks, he ticks off reasons why I should go back to Master-freaking-Lee's? Every single time. Not to mention his daily harassment in Math for Dummies. I'm sick of it. Sick of him. One-track Charlie. Chas the spaz."

Petra's cheeks burned. "He's just dedicated. Besides, it's his job."

"You call it dedicated. I call it fanatical." Jamie got up to throw away her leftovers. "Listen, Petra." She flopped back down and ran a hand through her curls, which glinted in the sun like copper wire. "Whatever you do, don't let Chas or that pinhead Todd talk you out of Running Start. You've got the smarts to go a long way fast, and you should do it."

"You're telling me that if you were in my place, you'd leave Belville High? Just like that?" Petra snapped her fingers. "What about art? What about music? Aren't you fighting now to stay in those classes?"

"They've got art and music at BCC, Pet. I only *wish* some counselor would give me the chance to jet out of here. She wouldn't have to ask twice."

Petra slumped against the bench. Now Chas would have to be the one to talk her out of early college. She'd need some pretty powerful arguments to convince her folks, because of course they wouldn't understand the importance of martial arts any more than Jamie did. It wasn't about taking a dare or winning a bet anymore. Not even about snagging a hot guy. Sometime in the last couple of months, the accelerated pace at Master Lee's had become a test of Petra's will, her inner strength, her endurance. She had a goal, a purpose only she could fulfill, and she simply *had* to fulfill it.

The silence stretched between her and Jamie until Petra remembered to ask, "How's your appeal going?"

"Okay, I guess." Jamie examined her nail polish. Pearl gray with gold stars. "I haven't heard anything lately. My advisor thinks the school board doesn't have a leg to stand on, changing rules in midstream. I hope she's right."

"Me, too," said Petra.

Jamie startled. "You mean it?"

"Well, sure." Petra set her lunch aside. "Why not?"

"I thought you wanted me back in hell—I mean Master Lee's. I thought you believed everyone, no matter who they are, should build character by suffering through a lifetime sentence there."

"Where'd you get that idea?"

"Your boyfriend."

"I told you, he's not my boyfriend." Five sodas and one occasion of hand-holding did not a boyfriend make.

"What is he, then?"

"He's—he's....I don't know. Just a friend, I guess."

"Well, whatever he is, he's telling me every chance he gets that *you* want me back at Master Lee's."

"What?" *How could he?* Petra had made it clear weeks ago that Jamie would never be happy at the school, no matter what Chas did to persuade her. "I mean I'd want you back if you were interested," she said. "You're my best friend and everything. It's fun to do things with you." *It used to be, anyway.* "But Chas must have gotten the wrong impression. I don't think Master Lee's is right for you."

Jamie eyed her skeptically. "So you don't think everyone should do martial arts?"

"Of course not. Only people who like it."

"Thank God. You're not one of *them*, then. There's still hope for you."

"What are you talking about?"

Jamie whirled so suddenly, Petra jumped. "Don't you see? You're letting yourself be played. That's how the cults get you. First they tell you what you want to hear, leading you on with bogus promises. Health, happiness, whatever. Then they tell you you've got to listen to them and do everything they say or something bad'll happen. Before you know it, you're a zombie."

Petra sighed. "Give me a break, Jamie. I know Sawhee Todd's over the top—one of those people who give a place a bad name—but Master Lee's is not a cult."

"Oh, yeah? Then why won't Chas leave me alone? Why do I get letters from the Todd squad—signed 'Yours in good health' by Lardbelly and Company—saying that if I don't come back, I'll be sorry?"

"Are you kidding? You got something like that in the mail?"

Jamie tossed her curls.

After a moment Petra said, "Can I see it?"

"Don't you believe me?"

"Of course I believe you! I just don't understand. I don't understand any of this." Petra pinched the bridge of her nose. The headache that had been brewing all morning felt like a migraine. "There must be some mistake. Maybe you misunderstood the letters. Maybe they just want you to know you're welcome to return if you change your mind."

"There's no mistake." Jamie grabbed Petra's arm. "Look, I know you think I'm jealous of you and Chas." She lowered her gaze. "And I *was* jealous at first. You're really good at martial arts, and I'm not. Plus Chas asked you out when I couldn't get to first base with him."

Petra opened her mouth to say something, but Jamie's grip slid to Petra's wrist and she flinched instead. An inflamed arthritic lump on the back of her hand made the whole area extremely tender.

"Let me finish," said Jamie. "That's over now. I'm not jealous anymore, and I don't give a rip about Chas. I just wish he'd leave me alone. I wish he'd leave you alone, too. There's something wrong with him, and there's definitely something wrong with Todd. You have to get out of that place while you can." She squeezed tighter. "Please, Pet, I'm begging you. I'll even help you find another martial arts school. Today, if you want, right after orchestra."

Every muscle in Petra's body tensed. "Stop! You're hurting me." She pulled her hand away.

Jamie jerked back. "Sorry. My bad. You're flared up, aren't you?"

"I'm fine."

"You're not fine. You didn't eat anything for lunch, you're tired, and your hand hurts. Where else are you sore?"

Petra yawned. "How do you know I'm tired?"

Jamie cocked her head, blue eyes wide, until Petra cracked a sheepish smile.

"One more thing and I'm done," said Jamie. "I think you're selling yourself short—passing up a great opportunity to get ahead in life, acting like your only chance for happiness is at Master Lee's, and totally throwing yourself under a bus. I can't just stand by and watch that happen."

"Thanks for worrying about me, but I'm not selling myself short. I'm being careful. Thinking things through. Considering all my options."

Jamie shrugged. "It's your life, Pet. Just don't drink the Kool-Aid, okay?" She got to her feet shouldering her book bag.

Uncertain how to respond, Petra picked up her things and followed Jamie to class. Did that make her another sort of zombie, the kind that would rather eat crap than argue?

Her migraine worsened during Horseman's class—spots and squiggles danced before her eyes when she looked at the board—and she missed most of the teacher's lecture. Again. Master Lee's couldn't be a cult, Petra told herself. It had done too much good for that. Jamie was still jealous, whether she realized it or not. She must be.

When the bell rang, Petra shoved her books in her bag and shot out the door without a word to anyone. She'd never before skipped school, and the strangeness of driving away from a fully packed lot gave her a sense of unreality overlaid with guilt. Good students didn't cut classes except in an emergency. Did this qualify as an emergency? It might if she went home sick.

She probably should go home, but the prospect depressed her. Lying in bed with an ice pack, wondering how much to tell her parents about Running Start versus Master Lee's. They still didn't know she'd switched from tai chi to a full spectrum of black-belt training. Somehow the right time to share that information had never presented itself.

Petra's cell buzzed. Glancing at the screen, she saw Jamie's name and didn't answer. She needed something more than conversation now. She needed action. The sun was out, the air sweet with the scent of spring flowers. Petra rolled down her window, pointed her car, and drove until she found herself at the large lakefront park where she'd first seen others going through the graceful motions of tai chi.

She maneuvered into a slot marked COMPACT and zipped her keys into her backpack. Sunlight slanted through the windshield. The glare made her eyes water. She climbed out of the car, disappointed not to see the tai chi group even though she understood they couldn't practice all the time.

Two women exchanging remedies for diaper rash pushed strollers across the lawn toward the lake. A tall man jogged by on the pavement, sweat flying off his face. Shrieking preschool children writhed over the playground equipment while an old couple, hard of hearing, sat on a bench and shouted at each other. It shouldn't be this way, Petra thought. It should be peaceful, quiet, serene.

She took her time searching out a secluded area. Inland from the waterfront, she caught the cloying odor of a lilac past its prime and sneezed. Everything had grown so intensely green and bright. Red-winged blackbirds pierced her skull with their shrill whistles. Insects buzzed around her head. In a spot sheltered on three sides by high hedges, she dumped her backpack and hoodie under a tree, then climbed a slight knoll to a level expanse of lawn. There she launched her warmup routine.

She soon became immersed in the movements. Stepping. Gliding. Twisting. Turning. Punching. Kicking. She practiced until perspiration streamed from her face and every joint ached. She didn't know what time it was. She didn't need to know. All that mattered was the form—perfecting the form with her wayward body. She couldn't let herself notice how much it hurt.

While she practiced, below the surface of her attention, a plan took shape. Petra circled her arms over her head, gathering *chi*. She would make an opportunity to talk to Dee LaGuardia as soon as possible. With a gentle thrust, she brought the *chi* down, crossed her arms over her chest, landed one foot behind the other, and came around with a slow-motion punch. Sensible, down-to-earth Dee would restore her faith in Chas and Master Lee's organization. She bent her knees and scooped up the *chi* near the ground.

After Dee, Petra would confront Chas himself about Jamie's accusations. She had no idea what he might say, but she felt confident he would have a logical explanation for the threatening letters and what Jamie called his "harassment" at school and at her place of employment. She released the *chi,* knowing that she couldn't make a decision about Running Start until she'd done those two things.

Petra returned to the beginning of her routine, determined to do better this time. Her motions had grown jerky. Now she concentrated on each segment. *Focus, don't think. Let it flow. Become one with the form.* Incredibly, her performance deteriorated even more. Jaw clenched, she put herself through the sequence over and over, flubbing one thing after another. At last, frustrated from messing up movements she'd learned weeks before, Petra collapsed on the grass, too exhausted to do any cool-down stretches. Overhead the sky wheeled. She closed her eyes against the spinning sun.

When she roused, soaked in sweat, her headache had eased somewhat, but as she shifted her position it felt like someone prodded her joints with a hot poker. She lay very still, willing herself to relax. The breeze chilled her, raising gooseflesh along her arms and legs. She had to get up. Rolling to one side, she pressed her fists into the grass and tried to lift up on her knees. Agonizing pain drilled into her wrists and shoulders. Stunned, she flopped back to the ground. She tried once more with the same results.

It took several minutes to admit to herself what had happened. For one thing, Petra didn't want to believe her disease had flared up. Not now. Not when she couldn't afford to be ill. A flare-up of this magnitude could set her back weeks. For another thing, she was hidden from passersby and far enough away from her cell phone that she might have to lie here for hours, struggling to rise and tumbling back in defeat.

"Somebody, help me," she shouted in a hoarse croak. After clearing her throat, she shouted some more, but no one came.

In time the sun disappeared behind a black cloud, casting sinister shades of sooty bronze over trees and grass. The wind kicked up. Petra shivered. With supreme effort, she eventually levered herself to her knees, every part of her body screaming in protest. A loud groan escaped her throat. It sounded weird and foreign to Petra, as if it had come from someone else. She rested on her knees, as much as she could rest, summoning strength for the next, more difficult push off the grass.

A wave of nausea threatened to spill what little lunch she'd gotten down. Her arms shook with the effort of supporting her upper body. Her knees hurt so bad that she bit her lip, tasting blood. A gust of wind knifed through her damp sweatshirt and jeans. Pain so intense that it sucked the breath from her lungs spiked up her weakened arms and toppled her.

There she lay, a few feet from her cell, panting like a dog. Completely helpless and utterly alone.

Chapter 15

"Are you all right?"

Petra squinted up into the face of an African-American woman in her late teens or early twenties. A baby in a stroller made fussy noises.

"I'm not sure." Petra's teeth chattered. She didn't know how long she'd been lying there, half praying, half out of her mind with fear and pain. The sky had darkened. Her clothes were wet. She felt cold and sticky. Gingerly, she stretched her legs. So far, so good. She attempted to lift up on one elbow. A fiery dart shot through her shoulder, but she managed not to fall back.

"Here, let me help you." The woman moved away from the stroller and squatted to offer a hand.

Petra shook her head. "I have to do it myself. It hurts less that way. Just—please don't leave me."

The woman straightened. "I'm not going anywhere."

Grunting and panting, Petra jockeyed herself off her back and onto her knees. It took a long time, and every few seconds she bit back the urge to cry out.

The infant in the carriage whimpered. Its mother, slender and dark in jeans and a denim jacket, rocked the stroller back and forth as she watched Petra. "I feel so useless," she said. "You sure I can't help you? How'd you hurt yourself?"

Petra gritted her teeth, too engrossed in her predicament to answer. She knew the final thrust was going to hurt like hell, and she had to steel herself for it. One pain-racked lunge and she'd be up. The trick would be staying up once she got there.

"Oh, ow! Ack! Ugh!" She stumbled to her feet.

The woman threw her arms out to steady her. "You okay?" She hovered nervously, bouncing on the balls of her feet.

"Mm." Petra reached behind to brush herself off, but her shoulders locked with warning pain.

"Here, let me." The woman dusted Petra down for grass and twigs. "Can I call someone for you?" She fumbled in a pocket for her cell phone.

"No," Petra said in a breathy voice. "But thanks. Thanks for your help." Dizzily she peered around for her backpack, spotting it where she'd left it under the tree with her navy hoodie on top. Too far to go without traversing a slippery slope, which she knew she couldn't do at the moment. "Um, I wonder if you could...."

As if reading her mind, Petra's rescuer jogged over to the tree and collected Petra's stuff. "You want to put your jacket on?"

Petra shook her head. It wouldn't be worth the pain to struggle into it.

The woman tied the hoodie to a strap of the pack and slung it over one shoulder. "Can you walk?"

"I think so."

"Where to? The bus stop?"

"Parking lot," Petra gasped.

Nodding, the young mother set off with the stroller.

Petra limped after her, moving as fast as she could, but a tortoise might have made better time. Her knees buckled whenever she forced speed.

"Sorry. I'll slow down." The woman waited for Petra to catch up, then eased the stroller over a bump and around a hedge to a well-worn path through the middle of the park. "Did you sprain something? I never would have seen you if I hadn't heard your moaning. Even then I was scared to check. You read all the time about rapists and muggers lying in wait, pretending to be injured."

"I'm glad you checked. No sprain. Nothing broken." Petra grimaced, every step jarring her joints, every word a drain on her small reserve of energy.

"That's good. By the way, I'm Lateesha Briggs." Lateesha stuck out her hand.

Petra hesitated. Some people's grips were murder during flare-ups. "Petra," she answered, tentatively extending her own hand.

"Oh, wow." Lateesha cradled it, running her thumb over the arthritic lump. "You're all red and swollen."

Petra nodded.

"You don't want to talk about it, do you?"

"Mm." She'd found it challenging enough to put one foot in front of the other. The parking lot seemed an impossibly long distance away.

"Gotcha," Lateesha said. "I'll shut up now."

When they finally arrived at Petra's little red convertible, Lateesha located the keys in Petra's backpack and unlocked the door for her. "You think you're safe to drive? I'd be happy to take you home, or call someone to come and get you."

"Uh-uh. I'm all right now. I don't know what I'd have done without you, though."

Tilting her head of tightly spaced corn rows, Lateesha studied Petra. "I'm glad I could help, but I'm not leaving until I know you're okay." The baby let out an impatient squawk, and Lateesha cooed to it.

"I'm fine," said Petra. "I was just practicing hard. Probably overdid it."

"Practicing what?"

"Martial arts."

"Oh." Lateesha opened the passenger door and stowed Petra's things. "Are you one of Mr. Pang's group? I've never seen you here before."

"You mean the people who practice on the waterfront?" Petra shook her head. "I'm a student at Master Lee's School of True Martial Arts."

"Master Lee's? I think my brother tried that place early in his search for a tai chi instructor. If I remember right, he said the teaching was harsh." Abruptly, she closed her mouth. "Sorry. Hope I didn't offend you."

"No. Master Lee's *is* demanding. You know. Work hard. No pain, no gain. Stuff like that."

"Oh, okay. No wonder Darnell didn't go for it. He had to drop out of track because he kept reinjuring his Achilles, and he wanted something that would keep him in shape and calm him down at the same time." She laughed. "He's pretty ADD."

"ADD?" Petra repeated politely.

"He hasn't been diagnosed with attention deficit or anything. I just call him that because he's always on the go, you know? Sort of an inside joke. Anyway, the teacher he settled on is a sweet old Chinese man who likes his students to practice outdoors when they can—to get 'tuned to the earth and the elements.' I like him a lot. In fact, I plan to join the group as soon as Amariana's old enough to be left with a sitter. They practice every Monday, Wednesday, and Saturday afternoon. Here if it's decent out, at the community center if the weather's bad. Mr. Pang teaches meditation and breathing techniques, too."

"That's nice." Petra didn't know what else to say. Her body ached, and her head felt like it had split down the middle. "Well, thanks again."

"No problem." Lateesha handed her the keys. "Oh, and here's my number if you need anything. Or in case you'd like to join Mr. Pang's group." She scribbled something on a card she'd taken from her pocket.

Petra accepted the card reluctantly. What was it about martial arts people that made them worse than religious nuts, trolling for converts, proclaiming their brand the best or the truest? Carefully backing up to the driver's seat, she dropped down sideways with a yelp. Her legs refused to bend or to swing inside, so she tugged at them with her inflamed hands.

Lateesha lifted Petra's feet. "There," she said, tucking them inside the car. "Take care, and don't practice so hard next time."

Hiding her irritation at being nagged, Petra thanked Lateesha again as the young woman shut her door for her. Then she switched on the ignition, revved the motor, and backed out using only her mirrors. Her neck was too stiff to twist. Lateesha stood watching her out of sight, one hand on the stroller and the other shading her eyes from the reflected glare of a peek-a-boo sun.

No question of Petra's attending her black-belt class today. She could barely hold her head up, let alone an arm or a leg. She sighed, already rehearsing excuses for Chas which alternated between downplaying her illness and spilling the whole story. At home she parked next to her father's Mini and contemplated the ordeal of getting out of the car, into the house, and up the stairs to bed. Maneuvering out of the driver's seat felt like torture. She slumped against a dusty fender until she could muster the strength to let herself into the rectory.

To her surprise, Alf, the Merry Moppette, was in the kitchen making coffee. She saw the clock. Almost 4, even though she'd left Belville High shortly after lunch. Now it came back to her that she'd agreed to go home right after school to pay Alf, because her father had used his last check and forgotten to reorder. Could she have practiced that long? Could it be that she'd lain unconscious for hours before Lateesha found her? She shivered. She didn't know, but damp and chill had settled into her bones.

"Hello there, Miss Petra." Alf's grin revealed uneven, tobacco-stained teeth. His yellowish gray hair had been scraped back to a short pigtail. "I put in extra time waiting for you. Your dad said on the phone you'd make it good." He pried the lid off his thermos and poured coffee inside. A few dregs remained in the pot when he looked up. "You wouldn't want any of this, would you? You look beat."

"I am." Petra hobbled toward the living room. She made it to her father's recliner before a rush of light-headedness hit.

"Anything I can do for you before I go?" Alf trailed her, clutching his Mariner's cap and a broom.

Petra figured the broom was a prop. He'd most likely

knocked off work hours ago. "I'm not feeling well," she said. "Would you call my father at the church?"

"Sure thing." Alf put on his hat, angled the broom against the wall, and reached for the receiver succumbing to a fit of smoker's cough.

Petra let the spasm subside before she spoke again. "You can go home after that. I'll have Daddy mail you a check." No way could she make it to the household cash hidden in the laundry room.

Alf raised his eyebrows, the color draining from his face.

Worried about losing his cushy job, Petra guessed. If she'd had more energy, she might have reassured him. As it was, she just didn't care. Not about Alf. Not about the rectory or whether it was clean. Not about anything, except getting beyond this hideous pain and exhaustion. Her eyelids drooped. The next thing she knew, her father took her hand.

"You're like ice, my dear."

"Am I?" His hand felt hot.

"Can you manage the stairs? You should get out of those wet things."

"I'll try." Petra willed herself to slide out of the chair. Her clothes stuck to the leather, and her muscles were as useless as jelly. Even tiny movements caused her to gasp with pain. Tears welled in her eyes. When she looked into her father's face, she saw tears there, too.

"Well, love," he said softly, "I had hoped I'd never have to do this again." He indicated he would pick her up.

"Oh, Daddy, I'm too heavy now."

"Nonsense. Brace yourself. I'll be as gentle as I can."

She did, and he was. Upstairs, he paused at the threshold of her bedroom. "Shall I put you down by the dresser or the closet?"

"On the bed, please. I can't change my clothes right now."

"But you're soaked through and shivering with cold!"

"Can't help it. Pile on the blankets and I'll get warm." Petra knew from experience that she wouldn't be able to shift around much once she got down, so she asked Peter to fluff her pillow as well. Although thirsty, she refused his offer of water. Until she got some rest, she couldn't negotiate the toilet without her father's help, and that was too weird to consider.

He removed her shoes and socks before he tucked extra blankets and a heavy comforter around her. "Hot water bottles would do nicely," he said. "Where are they kept?"

"Bathroom, under the sink." Petra drifted off in spite of her frozen feet and hands. She almost resented the intrusion when her father returned. She welcomed the warmth of the bottles but didn't enjoy the feel of rubber on her skin. Peter hadn't thought to wrap them in towels.

"I've brought oil, my dear."

"Oil?" Petra's eyes fluttered open.

He held up his bottle of holy oil. "May I anoint you and pray?"

"Mm." Prayer couldn't hurt, but she wished he'd get on with it and let her sleep.

Her father's oily thumb touched her forehead. She felt him make the sign of the cross. He intoned a petition for healing from the *Book of Common Prayer*. Then she heard him whisper something else. Something about "beautiful daughter" and "tender mercy."

She stirred. "Thank you, Daddy."

"I'm going to ring your mother now, but I'll be back straight away. Are you strong enough to shout if you need me?"

Petra thought about answering, but the words were too far from her tongue.

"Perhaps not," he said. "I'll find the little bell we used before, shall I?" Her father lingered at her side.

Petra sensed his anxiety. She wished she could comfort him.

Turning her head, she snuggled deeper into her pillow, groaned with the effort, and slid into a lucid dream in which she rode Attaboy. She knew it was a dream, but she enjoyed the images and sensations so much that she let them unfold without interference. A warm wind blew across her face, making her laugh with delight. She clung to Attaboy's mane, her own hair streaming out behind her, free and easy. At some point, the horse sprouted wings and flew her over housetops and busy streets to Master Lee's. There she astounded everyone by performing so well that SAAHI Todd took off his own black belt and respectfully tied it around her waist.

She jerked awake when her father put the bell—an old Christmas ornament—on her nightstand. The contrast between dream and reality sliced into her awareness like a dull razor, and she squeezed her eyes shut while her father fussed over her. When she didn't respond to any of his questions, he pulled the curtains and tiptoed out.

Chapter 16

Petra woke up with her bladder ready to burst. She tried to roll over and groaned. Her shoulders would not support her. In the half-gloom of her darkened bedroom she caught sight of the bell her father had placed on the night table. An excruciating attempt to grasp it sent the ornament crashing to the hardwood floor.

To Petra's relief, her mother appeared at the door.

"Darling, how are you?" Catherine came to the bed and laid a cool hand on her daughter's forehead. "We've been so worried. I just dashed out for a minute." She gestured toward the chair where she'd been sitting. "Oh, sweetie, you're burning up." She crossed to Petra's dresser, picked up a pitcher of water, and filled a glass.

Petra shook her head. "Not yet. I have to use the bathroom."

"All right." Catherine put down the glass and retrieved the little bell. "I'll help you up."

Catherine lifted while Petra floundered, biting her lips to keep from screaming.

"Let me rest for a second." Petra panted on the edge of the

bed. When her pulse slowed and she felt able to face the ordeal, she said, "Okay, I'm ready."

"Your father found your old crutches in the basement." Catherine pointed to the corner by the door. "He adjusted them to my height, since you and I are the same now."

"No crutches," Petra muttered. During her last big flare-up, she had used one or the other of the aluminum sticks to steady herself when moving from bed to toilet. Stabs of pain lanced through her knees now as she put weight on her feet. Still, using a crutch would be like giving in to a long siege of illness. She didn't have time for that. She had to test for third section in a few days.

Petra shuffled down the hall, her mother holding her around the waist, careful not to press or pull on any of the joints in Petra's upper body. This meant Petra had to crook her inside arm in front of her at an awkward angle. She felt faint by the time they got to the bathroom. Heart racing, she sagged against the counter while sweat poured out of her.

A booster seat had been unearthed and placed on the toilet. She decided not to fight that like she fought the crutches. Petra knew very well she'd never get off an ordinary toilet seat by herself, even if she managed to collapse on it in the first place without breaking her tailbone.

"Do you need help with your pants?"

Petra screwed up her face. Would her mother have to wipe her butt, too? Some wild energy, half anger, half determination, surged through her body. "I need privacy," she said with more vehemence than she intended.

"Fine," her mother said mildly. "I'll wait outside."

Petra nodded. Every movement was a tedious, racking chore. Shut inside the bathroom, she suppressed her groans, knowing

Catherine listened at the door. It took ages to unzip her jeans, which she left on the floor of the bathroom. Getting on and off the toilet constituted another lengthy operation. Her hips, knees, and shoulders howled in protest.

Catherine called out, "Darling, are you okay?"

"Yes." Petra inched her way to the sink. "I'm washing my hands now."

She had so much inflammation in her wrists, she couldn't operate the faucet with one hand. Two hands for the cold water, two hands for the warm water, and even that hurt. Back in bed at last, all she could think of was more sleep. She ached all over as if she had the flu.

Catherine brought the water glass to her again. She took only enough to wet her tongue.

"You'll have to do better than that," said Catherine. "Remember last time you were so dehydrated, you wound up in the hospital."

Petra drank, more afraid of the hospital than of the agony entailed in getting to and from the bathroom.

"Good girl. Now finish it up."

She got most of it down before she sank into her pillow.

"I'm going to send Peter out for supplies," her mother said. "Juices, soft foods, ice cream. Oh, and we couldn't find the hospital bedpan. Do you know where it is?"

"Bedpan! Mother, I'm not that sick."

"You don't have to use it. I would just feel better knowing it's available."

Petra blinked back tears. "I think we got rid of it." She had a vague memory of packing the horrid thing, along with old toys and clothes she'd outgrown, in a box of donations for the Salvation Army.

"No problem," said Catherine. "I'll have Peter buy a new one from that medical supply store at the mall." She sat on the bed and pushed the matted hair from Petra's face. "I know it's hard, but it won't be forever. We'll get you through this, I promise."

I'll get through it all right, Petra thought. *But without a damn bedpan.* Her muscles tensed in defiance. After a few moments, though, she could no longer sustain the effort to be angry. The feathery caresses of Catherine's fingertips sent tingles down her spine. Her eyelids grew heavy. Mother's presence comforted her. Why did it have to take illness to bring her home?

Catherine continued her stroking. Petra slept.

* * *

She awoke to full dark. Light from the hall shone through a crack in her door. She tried to ignore her need for the toilet. Maybe, if she lucked out, she'd go back to sleep for a while. She shifted her body slightly. The covers weighed her down. Attempts to roll over tangled her in the bedding, and her arms hurt too much to free herself.

Unable to arrive at any sort of endurable position, she cried out. Catherine and Peter both rushed in, as if they'd been hanging around for just such a purpose. The hall light flooded over them like a double halo. In spite of everything, Petra's heart swelled with bittersweet satisfaction to see her parents side by side.

"What time is it?" she asked.

"Just gone eleven," said her father.

"At night?"

"Yes," her mother confirmed. "We hated to wake you when you were sleeping so soundly. How about some dinner?"

Petra wrenched her head away. "I'm not hungry."

"Nonetheless," put in Peter, his voice falsely cheerful, "we'll not have any daughter of ours going without food and drink."

"Speaking of which...." Catherine went to the dresser and poured another glass of water. "We're not letting you get dehydrated either."

She gestured for Peter to raise Petra's head. He straightened her covers first and pulled them tight. Feeling like a mummy swathed in bandages, Petra swallowed the tepid liquid in spurts.

As soon as Peter left to microwave Petra's dinner, Catherine asked if she wanted the bedpan, which she pulled from a white plastic shopping bag.

"Bathroom," said Petra.

"All right, sweetie. But if it's too much, you let me know." Catherine tucked the bedpan out of sight.

This time Petra thought it seemed fractionally easier to stand. She moved a shade more rapidly. And, best of all, she discovered she could bend her knees a little.

"Mother, I feel better already," she announced when she lurched out of the bathroom.

"Wonderful, darling." Catherine helped her back to bed. She'd arranged pillows against the headboard so Petra could sit up.

Petra fell against them, short of breath but enormously happy to see progress so soon. Maybe she'd be her old self again in a day or two.

"Here we are." Her father breezed in with a tray. "Drumstick, mash and gravy, milk, custard." He set the tray across Petra's lap, then went in search of another chair.

"KFC," said Catherine. "Your father, Zeke, and I ate earlier."

Petra looked at the unappetizing tray. Normally she loved these foods—what her dad called custard was really chocolate pudding—but tonight they might have been sawdust for all the pleasure she would take in gagging them down. Regardless, she picked up a fork, intent on getting through everything. Healthy people eat to keep up their strength. Healthy people think positive, according to Master Lee. If that's all it took to rise from her sickbed and get on with her life, she would do nothing but think prescribed thoughts. She would recite Master Lee's words of wisdom backwards and forwards until she literally glowed with health. *Push through the pain to the gain.*

Petra ate a mouthful of mashed potatoes. "Where's Zeke?"

"In bed," said her mother. "Here, in his old room."

"Does that mean you're staying overnight, too?"

"Of course, darling. I'll be right next door in the guest room for as long as you need me. By the way, you got three phone messages on the landline. I imagine you'll want to check your cell, too."

"Who from?" Petra held her breath, certain she knew the source of at least one.

"Mom—your grandmother." Catherine began ticking the messages off on her fingers. "Actually, I phoned her first. But she called back an hour ago to see how you were doing. She sends her love, and we're supposed to give you a big hug as soon as you're well enough."

Petra understood that Grandma Morse would be here if she could, but her own arthritis had worsened to the point of needing assisted living. She seldom left her home at a seniors' apartment complex in Seattle any more.

"She also told me to tell you to go back to your vitamins and supplements."

Petra choked on her milk. "How does she know I went off of them?"

"She knows. She said to increase the turmeric and fish oil. Is there something else you take? Something called Modern Care?"

"Moducare." Petra didn't want to think about that now. She'd have to get a new prescription from her naturopath. "Who else called?"

"Jamie. She worried when you left horsemanship class so abruptly?" Catherine's voice trebled into a question. "I don't remember hearing about any equestrian training after Attaboy." She wagged her finger at Petra. "You're simply not going to finagle a horse out of me, young lady. I won't even let Zeke have a dog."

Petra stared at her, suddenly reliving her flying-horse dream and trying to make the connection to this conversation. "Oh, Mother," she said after a moment. "Horseman's our history teacher. His real name's Chevalier."

Catherine grinned.

"You knew that, didn't you?"

"Had you going for a minute, didn't I?" She winked.

Petra indulged her mother with a smile, but she was eager to get on to more important things. "Did you say three people called?" The third one had to be Chas. She'd never missed a lesson before, and he would be worried.

Her father entered the room with a folding chair. "I stumbled across a whole set of these in the basement looking for the crutches. It's been a long time since we had a bridge party, hasn't it, Cat?"

Petra thought he sounded wistful. She looked to see if his words had touched her mother.

Catherine merely scooted her chair closer to the head of the bed to make room for Peter before she answered Petra. "Your father took the call. Maybe he should tell you." She turned to her ex-husband. "Petra wants to know who phoned besides my mother and Jamie."

"Oh, yes, that odd message." Peter lowered himself onto the folding chair. "It came in—oh, I couldn't say, really, but after I rang your mother. From the high school guidance office. Something to do with a jump start?" He scratched his thinning scalp. "Well, anyway, it seems there's a deadline. She said you'd know what it's about."

Petra's fork clattered to the tray. "Daddy, I need you to get my cell phone out of my backpack. It's in the car."

Peter looked surprised, but he got up to go.

"What's the emergency?" Catherine asked after Peter left the room. "The school counselor won't be in now."

Petra shrugged. Took another small bite of food. Fought to keep it down. Gazed toward the window.

"Sweetie?" Catherine touched her hand. "Are you okay?"

"Just tired."

"You rest then. I'll talk."

Petra put her head back and closed her eyes. She didn't need to do anything but pretend to listen while her mother told a humorous story about a new client who wanted to decorate an upscale restaurant lobby with garden gnomes.

In her heart Petra nurtured a small hope. She had given Chas her cell number a couple of weeks ago. He hadn't exactly asked for it, but she had pressed it on him anyway, urging him to call her with news of test schedules. She'd been disappointed when he didn't reciprocate with his own number. He'd never called, either. She had to read the postings outside the practice room like everyone else. But maybe now…?

Peter clumped into the room with her backpack. "Where do you want this?"

"Anywhere. On the floor," said Petra. "The cell's in the front pocket."

When Peter handed her the phone, she smiled awkwardly at her parents. "Thanks for everything. You've both been awesome. I—well, I'd like to listen to my messages. Do you mind?"

"Of course not," answered Catherine. Briskly, she removed Petra's tray, leaned over, and kissed her daughter's hot forehead. "Ring the bell when you want me. We'll leave the door open a crack."

"Thanks." Petra watched them out, then quickly glanced through her messages. Three from Jamie. Two from her biology lab partner. One from the high school guidance office. One from Reverend Elisabeth at the church. Her father must have said something when Alf called. Petra scrolled through the list of messages again, this time more slowly. Then, without listening to any of them, she tossed the phone aside.

Nothing from Chas. Not a word. He didn't miss her at all.

Chapter 17

Petra did not get well as soon as she'd hoped, in spite of massive doses of positive thinking and tedious efforts to visualize herself back at Master Lee's each time she shut her eyes. She spent a week in bed with gradually diminishing pain and the virus-like symptoms characteristic of severe rheumatoid arthritis.

Although she missed three more black-belt classes, she didn't hear from Chas. Or from SAAHI Todd. So much for Jamie's accusation that the instructors at Master Lee's badgered dropouts to come back. For all they knew, Petra could have switched to another martial arts program, joined the circus, or simply fallen off the face of the earth. Did they care? Apparently not. This frustrated and depressed her even more than the slow progress of her recovery.

During that week Petra's mother brought her meals at which she picked with little appetite, helped her up and down whenever she had to get out of bed, and sat beside her for hours talking or sketching decorating plans. Sometimes Catherine showed her the designs and asked her opinion of layouts or color schemes. Petra, who considered herself lacking in artistic talent, nevertheless felt pleased to be consulted, especially when her mother took her views seriously. From the time she arrived to nurse Petra until the day she went home, Catherine did all her work from the rectory and left the house only to run Zeke to and from school and his other activities.

Achy and bored while alone, Petra slept, channel-surfed a portable TV, played computer solitaire, did homework via email, and explored new websites using Catherine's laptop. On impulse she Googled Master Lee's School of True Martial Arts and learned that a new school had just opened in Vancouver, B.C. SAAHI Todd and Instructor Franklin were there for the ribbon cutting. She also found a blog that posted comments about Master Lee's string of franchises and his approach to martial arts.

The blog responders fell into two camps. The minority praised Master Lee to the sky. One signed CAL in WA, might have come from Chas. CAL could stand for Chas A. LaGuardia. But the majority of the writers, by a three-to-one margin, had complaints. Petra read accusations against schools in Pennsylvania, Florida, Arizona, and California as well as Washington. Classes were overpriced, instructors unrealistic about what the program could do for students, and the discipline too strict.

Petra reread the posting from CAL in WA. "FYI," it said, "Master Lee is for real. I'm not surprised that he's misunderstood by slackers like DZ in PA and KungFuGuy in FL. Anyone who does as much good as he's done is bound to be attacked by jealous individuals whose own efforts to improve themselves and the world fall short. Ignore them. Give Master Lee's an honest try. Practice, practice, practice. Obey higher belts. Reap the rewards. You won't be sorry."

Petra thought about adding her own voice to the mix, but she couldn't decide whether to repudiate the negative comments, as

CAL did, or to stick to her own experience. She wanted Chas to see her initials (PCG in WA) and realize how loyal she was. At the same time, it would be hard to extol the benefits of practice, practice, practice when overdoing it had landed her in bed. Still, too much of a good thing was better than not enough. At least that would be Master Lee's view. Maybe she'd wait to post anything until she recovered. Meanwhile, she bookmarked the site and checked it every day.

When Chas hadn't called by Friday morning, Petra sent word through Zeke that she'd been ill. Under normal circumstances, she would have done this earlier, but she was so mad at Chas for not calling after her first missed lesson that she told Zeke not to volunteer information about her to anyone at Master Lee's. She planned to find out how long it would take for someone to notice her absence, but she discovered that she hated being ignored, hated not knowing her status with Chas. Every time she thought of him, her guts churned. She had to force herself to be optimistic. There must be a reason, she told herself, and she'd hear it from Chas himself eventually. Even so, a niggling worry that he had forgotten her intruded on the peace of mind she worked so hard to achieve.

That afternoon her mother took a second message from the guidance office at Belville High. Unlike her former husband, Catherine pressed the counselor for details and confronted Petra about the Running Start program.

"Darling, why didn't you say something?" she asked Petra when she came back upstairs. Her musky perfume hung in the air after she sat down.

Petra fiddled with the TV remote, gauging how to tell her mother that concern for her academic future had fallen off the radar. Preoccupied by Chas's mysterious silence and driven to distraction trying to conjure up explanations for his neglect, she hadn't bothered to return her own call from the guidance counselor. The only message she'd responded to was from her lab partner, postponing a project meeting.

Jamie she'd put off with a text. Not that it kept her from phoning. Petra liked knowing how much Jamie cared, but conversations with her friend burned so much energy that she often let the VM pick up. Jamie wouldn't talk about Chas, anyway. The message from Reverend Elisabeth had been open-ended, assuring her of prayer and asking Petra to call if she wanted to chat. She did not. Not to Elisabeth, anyway.

"I don't know," Petra said in answer to Catherine's question about Running Start. "I got busy, I guess. Then sick." She slid down the polished-wood headboard, scrunching her pillow under her neck.

"But Petra, it's a wonderful opportunity! You must know that. Your father will be as happy for you as I am."

"Why?"

"Because we're proud of you. Proud of your achievements."

"What if I don't want to do it?"

Catherine poured Petra a glass of water. "I can't imagine why you wouldn't, but you know we've never forced you to do anything against your will."

"Except drink water." Petra turned to look outside, where she could see deep blue sky, fluffy clouds, and the top of a flowering hawthorn. After weeks of periodic rain and overcast, the weather had finally improved enough to open a window. The late afternoon sun slanted across Petra's bed, and a breeze lifted the curtains. Birds sang outside, but not for her. She was a prisoner in her own house.

"Do you want to talk about it?" asked Catherine.

"Talk about what?" Petra eyed her water glass with distaste.

"Running Start. Or whatever else is on your mind. I know something's bothering you."

"Well, of course something's bothering me!" Petra thrashed around to face her mother. "I want to be well. I want to go back to school. I miss martial arts. I miss—" She broke off, afraid of giving away too much.

Catherine crossed one elegant leg over the other. She had on cotton capris and a sleeveless print blouse, which she managed to wear with an air of casual charm. "Does it have anything to do with the young man who teaches you and Zeke at Master Lee's—the one you told me about in the restaurant? Zeke says it's obvious you're sweet on him."

"Sweet on him! What does Zeke know?"

"A lot, from the sound of it. Did you think you could hide your feelings from him? Or from anyone?"

Flushing, Petra set her mostly full glass on the nightstand. "His name is Chas. Chas LaGuardia."

"What kind of relationship do you have? I mean how has it developed?"

Petra wriggled around, trying to get comfortable. "We've gone to Starbucks a few times. He walks me to class if we run into each other on campus. He's all over my progress in martial arts. Stuff like that." Petra stopped short of confessing that he and SAAHI Todd had accelerated her program more than a month ago. Her parents didn't need to know now that she'd been working on a black belt.

"Has Chas ever phoned you?"

"No, but he has my number." Petra hunched forward to adjust her pillows and bit back a yelp.

"I see." Catherine fixed the pillows, smoothed the covers, handed Petra her glass. "You wonder why he hasn't called."

"Well, why hasn't he? It's as if I don't exist when I'm not there."

"Relax, sweetie. Stress isn't healing. I don't know why, but I could find out for you."

"You?"

"Yes, me. Drink up, please."

"I don't understand. What would you do?"

"Nothing to embarrass you." Catherine paused for effect. "I would simply collar your young man at the end of Zeke's next lesson and—"

Petra, who had been sipping water, sputtered and coughed. "You wouldn't! Oh, Mother, I'd die."

Catherine laughed. "Of course I wouldn't. I'd be subtle, I promise. I'd give him a progress report on you and see what he says."

Petra imagined the conversation. Mother: *So you've dumped my daughter.* Chas: *Huh? Who's that?* Mother: *Petra Cat Goodwyn, of course. Doesn't she resemble me?* Chas, squinting: *Not really.* Mother: *Well, call her anyway.* Chas: *Why?* Mother: *Because if you don't, I'll rip your face off.* Chas: *Oh. What's her number again?*

As suddenly as she'd conjured it, Petra dismissed the scenario. Catherine wouldn't threaten to rip anyone's face off. She'd simply shame Chas into doing her will. However, picturing her mother and Chas together reminded Petra of something she'd wanted to do before the onset of her flare-up.

"Mother," she said, "did I ever tell you Chas's mom is a

student at Master Lee's? She's really nice. She even showed me how to use fabric glue to shorten the jacket and pants of my uniform."

"And...?"

"Maybe I'll call her and see what the rule is at Master Lee's."

"Rule?"

"How they deal with students who're sick."

"There's a special rule about it? Sweetheart, we all get sick."

"I know." Petra shrugged, unwilling to go into detail about SAAHI Todd's strange ideas. "Would you bring me a phone book? I want to look up her number." She could dial 411, but she'd rather see for herself whether Dee used her whole name or her initials, and whether Chas had a separate listing.

Catherine stood. "I'll find it for you. The metro directory is not exactly light reading, and you don't need any extra strain on your joints. When you're finished with Chas's mother, let's have a talk about Running Start, okay?"

If we must. Petra waited impatiently as Catherine scanned the white pages for LaGuardias. She'd already figured out what she would say to Dee, how she would begin by asking what she'd missed over the past week.

"This must be it." Her mother reached for Petra's notebook and scribbled a number on the corner of one sheet. "LaGuardia, Deirdre. The address is not too far from Master Lee's."

"Deirdre?" Petra echoed. She'd never thought of Dee as short for anything. Chas's mom didn't look like a Deirdre to her. A Deirdre should be pale and slender, with wispy hair the color of moonlight. Come to think of it, did she, Petra, look like a Petra? Probably not, since she'd been named after her father, and she didn't look anything like him. She didn't look much like a cat either, although that was her middle name as well as her mother's nickname. "Is Chas listed by any chance?"

"Nope. No Chas, no Charles. Just Deirdre."

"How about C.A. LaGuardia?"

Catherine shook her head, eyes still fastened on the open directory.

"C with any other initial, or maybe just by itself?"

Her mother showed her the page in the phone book. "Satisfied?" she asked after Petra had searched the LaGuardias in vain for signs of Chas.

"Pretty much." Petra picked up her cell and looked pointedly at Catherine.

"Ring the bell when you're finished," her mother said, heading for the door.

Petra punched in the number, praying that Dee would be home. She noted the time. Almost 4:15.

Someone answered on the third ring. A male voice, but it couldn't be Chas's. He'd be at Master Lee's now, teaching Zeke's class.

"Who's this?" Petra blurted.

"Who are you calling?"

It *was* Chas!

Without thinking, she hit END.

Then she panicked. Deirdre might have Caller ID. Her stomach rolled before she remembered that she hadn't given her cell number to Dee but to Chas. He wouldn't recognize it away from his own phone, if he'd even taken the time to enter it there.

She gulped water and did some breathing exercises. When her heart quit pounding and a semblance of reason returned, she thought, Why shouldn't I talk to him, anyway? We're friends. We go to school together. He's my martial arts instructor.

She redialed and fidgeted while the phone rang and rang. She let it ring ten times, hung up, and tried again. Still no answer. Not even voice mail.

Disgusted with herself, she threw down the phone. Here she'd had Chas on the line—the answer to her questions at her fingertips—and she'd hung up.

What a ditz.

Chapter 18

After a week of bed rest, Petra got her parents to agree that she was well enough to return to school. Catherine and Zeke moved back to their condo on an unusually hot Tuesday evening in May. Before they left, Petra told Catherine she would drive her little brother to Master Lee's the following afternoon.

"All right," said Catherine. "I know you're dying to get back into the thick of things." She hugged Petra goodbye while Peter and Zeke loaded luggage into the Lexus. "But absolutely no practicing for you. You're not fully recovered yet."

"Like I haven't figured that out. It's my body, you know."

Catherine hefted a carryall she'd put down and turned to go, her jaw set.

"Mother," Petra said, "I'm sorry. I didn't mean to be rude. It's just—it's just that I'm going to miss you so much. Thanks for coming and staying with me."

"Of course, sweetie." Her mother dropped the bag and wrapped her arms around Petra. "I'll miss you, too. And here's a hug from your grandma. In all the excitement, I forgot to keep my promise. You *are* better, Petra—lots better. Anyone can see that. I only want you to give yourself the time you need to get all the way better."

"I know." Petra breathed in her mother's scent along with the porch smell of dust and old wood. The house's exterior needed painting. Would Catherine return this summer to supervise the painters, select their color blends, comment on the quality of their work? It might take some fast talking on Petra's part to convince her mother of the necessity, but she'd do what she could. She needed her here, even if the painters did not.

Catherine released Petra. "Call me." She picked up the carryall and descended the steps, disappearing around the corner to the driveway, where she'd parked.

The sun had dipped below the evergreens that separated the rectory from the churchyard. Shadows stretched across the sloping lawn, underscoring for Petra the melancholy mood of this parting. She wished for the thousandth time that she never had to say goodbye to Catherine. Or even to Zeke.

Her brother had been cagey about the reaction at Master Lee's after she allowed him to break the news of her illness.

"What did Chas say?" she wanted to know as soon as he got home that day.

"Nothing."

"Nothing?"

"Nothing about you. He said I'm scheduled to test for third section in a week."

Petra felt as though she'd been sucker punched. If she hadn't gotten sick, she'd have made third section already. "What about Sawhee—Seattle Area Associate Head Instructor Todd? What did he say?"

"Nothing. Can I go now?" Zeke obviously itched to get back

to his Wii boxing or whatever eleven-year-old boys did for fun.

"You're kidding. You told them both I'm sick and they said absolutely nothing? That's hard to believe."

Zeke shrugged.

"Nothing, as in not a single word? Not even *I'm sorry to hear that*?"

He remained silent, looking down and scuffing his Nikes together.

"Well, what did *you* say? Did you tell them I have a fever like I asked you to?"

"Yes! What more do you want?"

"Information would be nice. You're doling out words like food scraps in a famine." When Zeke didn't respond, she told him to go away. His face had split in a grin as he broke for the door, free at last. Self-absorbed little jerk.

Now she slumped on the porch swing, missing him already. In the distance she heard car doors slam. Catherine tooted her horn and took off with what sounded like a spray of gravel.

Moments later, her father climbed the porch steps. "Ha'penny for your thoughts."

"I'm not thinking. I'm sad."

Peter joined her on the swing. The wood creaked and groaned under his weight.

"I hate being sick," Petra said. "I hate that I had to take a whole week off from school and tai chi. But I loved having Mother here. Why can't she be here all the time?"

Peter patted her knee. "I expect if she were here, you wouldn't appreciate her nearly so much."

"Yes, I would."

"How much do you appreciate your old dad, then?"

"Oh, Daddy." Petra gave him a sideways hug, which tweaked her shoulder joint and made her flinch. They sat quietly together watching the sun sink and the shadows lengthen. A light breeze sprang up. Petra shivered.

"Oh-oh." Peter stood. "Into the house we go. Can't have you getting chilled."

Petra could have argued. The rapidly cooling air felt good on her bare arms. She'd been cooped up too long. But her parents were right. She did need to take extra care. It would be far too easy to imagine her body as ready as her mind to resume normal life.

She sighed. "I'm going to use your arm to pull myself up. Okay?"

"That's what it's there for." Her father gripped the swing carriage to steady himself.

The living room felt big and empty with just the two of them. Everywhere Petra turned she saw her mother's handiwork. Catherine had furnished the rectory in shades of rose and sage, with antique tables and accents to compliment the hundred-year-old house. Unlike other professionally decorated rooms Petra had seen, this one was attractive without calling attention to itself, a place where real people lived.

Petra couldn't help remembering the good times they'd had here when they were all together. The fireplace crackling or cheerfully filled with flowers from Catherine's garden. Catherine laughing, always laughing. Catherine poking fun at Peter until he, too, would laugh. Catherine surprising her and Zeke with a tray of cocoa and cinnamon rolls in winter, lemonade in summer. Catherine suggesting a four-way game of dominoes or Slap Jack, countering Peter's inclination to hole up alone in his study. Knitting four very different individuals into a unit by the sheer force of her personality.

Petra eased herself onto the sofa, overcome with nostalgia. Her father sat in his leather recliner. They gazed awkwardly at each other.

"Shall I switch on NPR?" Peter's hand hovered over the radio on the end table at his side.

"Sure." Petra's thoughts were too complicated for conversation, anyway. She wanted her mother back, and her father couldn't make that happen. Not that he tried very hard. No doubt Daddy did his best to cope with the divorce. Mother, too. They couldn't live their lives to please her, but it hurt to be split off from the whole family.

The radio boomed out Peter's favorite news program. Petra jumped.

"Sorry, my dear." Peter lowered the volume. "It appears your brother played with this earlier." He sat back in the chair, folding his hands over his stomach.

War in the Middle East. Earthquakes in Asia. Terrorist bombings somewhere. Petra's mind wandered. When would she be well enough to do martial arts? Why hadn't Chas called? Would she see him at school tomorrow, or would she have to wait until she brought Zeke in to Master Lee's for his lesson?

The phone shrilled, and Petra startled again. Her father hurried to answer it. She listened intently, but it was only one of Peter's parishioners. When he got off the line, Petra pleaded fatigue and went to bed early.

* * *

Although she and Jamie occupied their usual lunch perch the

next day at school, Petra didn't see Chas. The sun was hot, the air fragrant with new-mown grass. Petra wondered if six consecutive days without rain showers constituted some kind of record for spring in the Pacific Northwest.

When Jamie dashed inside to use the restroom, Petra fed the crows part of her sandwich and tossed her banana peel in the garbage. Then she flopped back down and lifted her face to the sky. Eyes closed, she listened to the starlings in a nearby bush. Farther away in the trees, squirrels chattered. Across the yard, a door banged shut. Petra's eyes flew open, but she didn't recognize the boy who loped across the quad to the cafeteria.

Jamie rejoined her on the bench. "It's so great to have you back, Pet."

"Thanks. And thanks for calling every day. I really appreciated it."

"No problem. Hey, how was trig this morning? I bet you couldn't do all your math homework over the Internet."

"You'd be amazed at what I can do on the Internet." Petra hesitated. "Speaking of math, did you and Chas talk much while I was gone?" She projected a casual tone, but her voice quavered.

Jamie pursed her lips. "Some."

"Some? What kind of answer is that? Jamie, I know you don't like Chas, but it's been driving me crazy all week. Did he or didn't he say anything about me?"

"You really want to know?"

Petra swallowed. "Yeah. Why not?"

"Okay." Jamie raised both her hands in surrender. "Not until yesterday when I asked him if he knew you were sick. He said Zeke had mentioned something about it. Then I asked if he had phoned you. He said, 'Not yet.'"

"Not yet?" Hope fluttered in Petra's chest.

"That's what he said. *Not yet.*"

"Then he *was* planning to call."

Jamie sighed. "I thought you might think that."

In a flash, Petra reviewed the week. Today was Wednesday. Her RA had flared up a week ago Tuesday. Although it seemed she'd been away from Master Lee's for months, it had been only eight days. Chas must have been busy at first. Then after he heard of her illness, he didn't want to disturb her.

"Did you tell him why I was sick?" she asked.

"No. Didn't Zeke?"

Petra shook her head. "I told him to say I had a fever—which I did—and that I'd be back at Master Lee's as soon as I could."

"If I were you," said Jamie, "I wouldn't pin your hopes on anything Chas LaGuardia did or didn't say. It's like I told you before. The only thing he cares about is martial arts. Period."

But Petra's heart said otherwise. She tucked her new perspective into a safe place, where she could pull it out and treasure it alone.

The first opportunity came after school at her mother's condo, while she waited for Zeke to log off the computer and change his clothes. By the time he got ready, she'd become so convinced of Chas's altruistic motives that she grinned to herself.

"What's so funny?" Zeke asked as he bounded into the living room dressed in his rumpled uniform.

"Nothing you'd understand." She wiped the telltale smile off her face. "Hey, don't you ever wash that thing? I can smell it clear over here."

"Shut up," he said.

"Shut up yourself."

"Make me."

She would if she could. Just to be contrary, Zeke began running his mouth a mile a minute. Petra didn't catch more than half of what he said on the drive to Master Lee's, but beating other kids at video games and sports contests figured prominently in his monolog. She yawned. Although tired, she looked forward to being back at the dojo and seeing Chas again.

Visitors were expected to observe lessons from the hall through a window at the back of the practice room. Within minutes of standing around, Petra longed to sit. Her first day out of bed, and already she felt drained from getting up early and going through the motions of a typical school day. Frustrated with her weakness, she dragged herself around the corner to SAAHI Todd's office.

Petra lingered for a full minute at the beaded curtain before he glanced up from his paperwork. Dutifully she bowed to the flags, then to him.

"Ain't seen you around lately," said the head instructor.

"I've been sick. Didn't Zeke tell you?"

His droopy left eyelid closed. "Go practice and you'll feel better."

"Practice?" Petra stepped backward. "I can't yet. I wondered, actually, if I could borrow a chair."

"What for?"

"To watch Zeke."

"Stand and watch like everybody else. Better yet, practice."

"But I can't! I promised my parents I wouldn't. I didn't even bring my uniform."

SAAHI Todd dropped his gaze, shuffling the papers in front of him.

Petra knew she'd been dismissed, written off as a slacker. For the first time since she'd joined Master Lee's, she refused to bow to an instructor. Propelled by anger, she wheeled about, marched to the women's room, and collapsed breathlessly on one of the benches. SAAHI Todd acted as if she were faking illness. Didn't he realize she'd give anything to be out there practicing her fool head off? Anything!

She stewed about the injustice of it all, her body buzzing with suppressed indignation. In spite of that, her eyes kept closing. Yawning hugely, she pulled a bag of clothes off the floor, made a pillow for her head, and lay down on her side. The bench's hard wood dug into her hip and shoulder, but she was too weary to care.

"Petra? Are you all right?"

Petra's lids fluttered open. Dee LaGuardia bent over her, her nose red and runny, her blond hair tangled. She wore a white tee shirt, jeans cuffed at her chubby knees, and green Crocs.

"Oh, hi." Petra tried to get up, grimaced with pain, grappled for leverage. She hoisted herself on one elbow and swung her feet to the floor.

Dee cleared her throat and spoke in a raspy voice. "Did you hurt yourself?"

"I've been sick."

"You, too? I wondered what was wrong when I didn't see you all last week."

"Didn't Chas tell you?"

"Tell me what?" After tossing her uniform on the bench, she fished in her purse for a tissue and sat across from Petra.

"I asked Zeke to let him know that I didn't feel well Friday. Sorry if you were worried."

"I was, a bit. But even if you'd said something earlier, I doubt he'd have told me. Chas keeps his job here completely separate from his home life." Dee blew her nose. "Gee, honey, you must have had it bad."

"Had what bad?"

"Whatever you had. You look tired."

Petra shoved the clothes bag she'd been using as a pillow to the floor. "I tried to call you last week."

Dee toed the bag into place under Petra's bench. "Oh? I didn't get the message."

"That's because Chas answered and I hung up."

Dee laughed. "He doesn't bite, you know."

"I know. It was just…weird. I wanted to find out if there's any sort of policy about instructors not contacting students when they don't show up for lessons because they're sick."

Dee stared past Petra to a spot on the wall. "One of the things I don't like about this place, is that you learn all the unwritten rules the hard way. No one tells you anything."

Petra's heart beat faster. "What do you mean?"

"I mean I don't know any more than you do. I have noticed, though, that the instructors—including Chas—talk as if illness can be overcome with practice. They recommend working even harder when you don't feel well." She covered her mouth to cough. "It was the same at the school in Phoenix, but I think Seattle Area Associate Head Instructor Todd is stricter than the head instructor there."

Petra sat forward. "What was Chas like before he took up martial arts?"

"Well, he's always been a good kid if that's what you're asking. Not like Seattle Area Associate Head Instructor Todd. Did Chas tell you how Master Lee rescued him from a gang fight in New Jersey?"

"Yeah, but he didn't say much about himself. Does Chas have any brothers or sisters? What does he do for fun? I mean, if you don't mind telling me."

"I don't mind. No sibs. Interested in athletics. Likes to read. Superhero comics in grade school, true stories about sports and nature these days. Loves animals. We used to have a dog—an Airedale terrier named Sammy. When he died, Chas, who was about twelve at the time, said he never wanted to do that again."

"Do what again?"

Dee shifted on the bench. "Get so attached, I suppose. Sammy had cancer, and we had to put him down. Chas wouldn't come out of his room for days after that. I...well, I got scared and called a child psychologist. Thank God he snapped out of it before the first appointment. Needless to say, I wasn't eager to rush out and buy another pet."

Petra got the picture of a sensitive boy who dealt with his vulnerabilities by walling them off mentally and developing physical defenses for good measure. No wonder Master Lee's philosophy appealed to Chas. It was all about being in control.

"Do you remember anything else?" she asked Dee.

"Let's see." She threw her head back to think. "He likes going to old car shows. Well, you know he drives a rebuilt Corvette. And he enjoys any sort of strategy game. He'd almost gotten to the point where he could beat his father at chess when—" She hesitated. "You know Chas's father and I are divorced?"

Petra nodded.

Dee rummaged in her purse for another tissue. "Chas took it pretty hard when his father moved out. I couldn't get him to talk about it, though. He just brooded, like he did after Sammy died. Chas wanted to go with his dad, but Charles Senior wouldn't hear of it. Peacemaker that I am"—she gave a self-mocking grunt—"I tried to make Charles's decision seem more like my unwillingness to let Chas go. You know, for Chas's sake. He misses his father terribly."

"He does?" Petra straightened up. Chas hadn't let on as much to her. SAAHI Todd and Master Lee were his fathers now. Or so he'd said.

"Of course he does." Dee narrowed her eyes, challenging Petra's sanity. "Wouldn't you?"

Petra hurried to correct herself. "I didn't mean it that way. I meant—it's just that—well, I got the impression from Chas that he'd gotten over the divorce pretty fast."

"Don't you believe it, honey. That's just an act." Dee got up to toss her used tissues into the restroom trash can. "I celebrated when Chas got involved at Master Lee's. It pulled him right out of his grand funk. Gave him something to work for. And it's such a blessing that there's a Master Lee's in Belville. I was afraid that after we left Phoenix he would spiral down into another depression."

So Chas gets as bummed over the split in his family as I do,

Petra thought.

Dee reseated herself. "Sometimes I worry about my son going overboard with martial arts. I hardly know him anymore, he's so businesslike. As if he's an instructor twenty-four, seven. But it's taken his mind off his dad, so I can't complain." She studied her shoes. "You can probably tell I've got a bad case of mother's guilt. I feel one hundred percent responsible for the divorce, even though it was only half my fault. The truth is, when it comes to the kids in a broken family, it doesn't matter who's to blame. They suffer the consequences either way."

Tell me about it, Petra agreed silently. She hoped Dee would go on, but the older woman stood, taking more tissues from her purse.

With another swipe at her raw nose, she said, "Guess I'd better go practice now if I'm going to knock out this cold."

Petra stirred. "You believe you can do that?"

"Well, I guess I don't *disbelieve* it. Chas hasn't been sick a day since he walked into Master Lee's. It won't hurt me to see if I can sweat this thing out."

"Good luck." Petra stumbled to her feet.

"You seem awfully sore, honey," said Dee. "It's not flu, is it?"

Petra shook her head, focused on angling toward the door without limping. "I had a sort of relapse. Thanks, Dee."

"Relapse from what?"

"From—an old problem, but I'm better now. I gotta catch Zeke."

Dee sneezed. "Maybe we should both be home in bed."

No way. Been there, done that.

From the viewing area Petra saw Zeke and five other boys and girls go through their cool-down stretches under Chas's guidance. Chas looked so hot in his black-trimmed uniform that her heart melted into a warm puddle. If she could stay on her feet long enough, Chas might invite her next door for a soda while Zeke practiced after the lesson. He might even explain why he didn't call.

Dee came to the curtain on Petra's left and waited for Chas to bow her in. Petra waved to her through the window. Dee waved back before reaching for one of a handful of tissues tucked into her belt. If Petra had brought her uniform, she'd be in there practicing as well, promise or no promise. She ached to participate.

Light-headed from standing too long, Petra shifted her weight back and forth as she waited for Chas to end the lesson. But when Zeke and the other students trooped out of the practice room, Chas exited on the other side, near SAAHI Todd's office. Petra slid to the floor with her back against the wall.

She half fretted, half dozed until Zeke and his friends piled out of the men's locker room dressed in civilian clothes. "What are you doing down there?" he asked Petra.

"What does it look like I'm doing? Go wait at the car. I'll be out in a minute."

He made a farting noise at which the other boys laughed, then led the charge around the corner to SAAHI Todd's office.

Petra ignored him, preoccupied with her own concerns. She felt sure that Chas had seen her at the window. Their eyes met more than once, but he never acknowledged her, and now he was hiding in the office. It didn't make any sense. She had done nothing wrong. Besides, such cold behavior seemed out of character with the boy Dee had described, the boy Petra had gotten to know a little.

Why would Chas treat her like a pariah all of a sudden? Why look right through her as if she weren't there? Painfully, she struggled to her feet.

She had to find out. Now, before her courage deserted her.

Chapter 19

SAAHI Todd peered at Petra through the beaded curtain. "You walked off earlier without bowing to me."

"Did I?" Petra bowed. "May I speak to Chas?"

"Assistant Instructor Chas to you."

"Sorry. Assistant Instructor Chas. Is he here?"

SAAHI Todd's eyes darted to the right, confirming Petra's suspicion that Chas stood or sat just out of view in the office. "Will you be in for your lesson tomorrow?" the head instructor asked when his piercing gaze returned to Petra.

"If I can. I'm still pretty tired." Why was Chas avoiding her?

"You better. I already put off your third-section test for a month."

Petra stared at him. "Why? I've only been gone a week."

"When you don't show up, it sets you back. Three to four weeks for every week off."

"But I got sick. I'll make up for what I missed."

SAAHI Todd opened a drawer in his desk and rummaged

through it. Clearly, he meant to dismiss her without further comment, but Petra refused to be dismissed. She would stand here all day if she had to.

She swayed with fatigue by the time SAAHI Todd looked up again, his brows puckered ominously. "Whatcha waitin' for? We're done here."

To her left, Petra heard a shuffle and a quiet clearing of the throat. She summoned her courage. "May I speak to Assistant Instructor Chas?"

"He ain't here for you to speak to." Once again SAAHI Todd's eyes shifted to the corner, belying his words. "Listen," he added, closing the drawer and giving her his full attention. "I seen what you can do when you put your mind to it. I don't want no sloughin' off, see? I wouldn't be doin' you no favor to let that happen. Now go on home, but be here tomorrow. I'll keep tabs on your lessons, and if I judge you can do it, I'll reconsider the delay. Maybe only one or two weeks instead of three or four."

Petra's head swam. She still didn't know why she couldn't talk to Chas, but she needed to get off her feet. She also needed a good night's rest if she wanted to show SAAHI Todd—and Chas—she hadn't wimped out on her commitment.

"Thank you, Seattle Area Associate Head Instructor," she said through clenched teeth. "I'll see you tomorrow." She bowed to the flags, then to SAAHI Todd. On a whim, she rotated to her left and bowed to the invisible Chas as well.

Zeke sat on the sidewalk next to her car. "Freakin' hell," he said, jumping up. "I thought you'd never come out. It's hotter than a witch's tit out here."

Petra made a face. "You know Mother and Daddy don't like you to talk like that."

"Talk like what?" Zeke used the bottom of his sweaty tee

shirt to mop his freckled face. The spikes in his sandy hair had wilted to half-mast. "There's nothing wrong with a witch's tit. Not if you're a witch's baby, anyway."

"For your information, the expression is *colder* than a witch's tit."

"But it's hot out here, not cold."

"Yes, but the expression is—oh, never mind! Get in the car."

Petra climbed into the driver's side with care. Her knees didn't bend easily. How could she do her best tomorrow when she wasn't fully recovered from her flare-up and SAAHI Todd would be breathing down her neck? She tore out of the parking lot with a squeal of tires.

Clutching the dashboard, Zeke bellowed, "Whoa! What's that about?"

"Nothing."

"Seemed like something to me." After looking around suspiciously, he settled back in his seat. "Assistant Instructor Chas said I'm in good shape for my test Friday."

"Well, big ups for you. You don't have to brag about it."

"I'm not bragging!"

"Are too."

"Dee two."

"Very funny. Master Luke would be proud."

"You mean Master Lee."

"No, I mean Master Luke. You're the one who wants to play *Star Wars*."

He smirked. "You're just jealous 'cause I'm testing ahead of you."

Petra took her eyes off the road long enough to glare at her brother. "In your dreams. I could be testing tomorrow, for all you know."

"No way." Zeke's grin displayed the gap between his two front teeth.

"Yes. Way."

"Liar. I know you're not testing before me."

"You don't know a bloody thing about it."

"Now look who's using bad words!"

"One word. Bloody. And it's only bad in England."

"So? Dad wouldn't like it."

"Daddy would wring your neck if he had to listen to you all day long. Now shut up."

"You shut up. I'm testing before you, and there's nothing you can do about it. Assistant Instructor Chas said so."

"He did not."

"Did too. Just a few minutes ago."

"What, during your lesson? How did my name come up?"

"Wouldn't you like to know?"

Petra whipped into the Safeway lot, switched off the ignition, and twisted sideways, ignoring pains in her hip and shoulder. "You think you're getting to me with this childish teasing? You think I don't know Chas—Assistant Instructor Chas—at least as well as you do? I know he doesn't discuss one student's business with another." If what Dee said about him was true, anyway. And why wouldn't it be true? His mother ought to know Chas better than anyone else.

"Then how come I know you won't be testing until a month from now?"

Petra recoiled as if she'd been slapped. "You don't. You're making it up."

"I'm right, ain't I?"

"Okay, then, tell me exactly what Chas said."

"Why should I?" Zeke folded his arms over his chest.

Petra glowered at him. "Tell me what he said, or I'll...."

"You'll what? Chase me on crutches? Run over me in a wheelchair?"

"You—you're despicable."

"Oh, yeah? You're the one who's des...des—what you said."

Petra smiled. She'd finally gotten the best of Zeke.

"What's so funny?"

"You are."

"Not either," muttered Zeke, obviously deflated.

Petra backed out of the supermarket parking lot. She could relax now, confident that whatever Chas had told her brother, it didn't involve her. Zeke's alleged intel about the month's delay was just a lucky guess.

Zeke crossed his arms over his chest with a loud chuff.

Petra glanced to the side. "What's that about?"

"Nothing."

"Come on, what is it?"

Zeke uncrossed his arms and looked at her. "I told you the truth and you don't believe me. Assistant Instructor Chas really did tell me you're not testing for a month."

Petra slipped into a break in traffic. "I'm listening," she said after a pause. "What did he say?"

"Like I told you. Quote. 'Your sister missed a week. She won't test for another month. You'll be a third section before she is.' Unquote."

Her heart sank. Zeke's words had the ring of truth. "But why would he say anything to you about it?" she asked. "It's none of your business. Besides, he told Jamie and me martial arts isn't about competing with other people."

Zeke lifted his shoulders.

"And those were his actual words?"

"No, Jackie Chan's words. Lay offa me, will ya? I told you what you wanted to know."

Petra tightened her grip on the steering wheel.

"This ain't the way home," said Zeke.

"It's a shortcut," Petra lied. She signaled to change lanes. "And don't say *ain't*."

"Why not? Seattle Area Associate Head Instructor Todd says it."

"That don't make it right." Petra bit her lip. "Now look what you've done! You've got me copying him."

"Ain't it fun?'

Petra didn't answer, her brain busy with the mystery of Chas. Just when she thought she had him figured out, he did something totally incomprehensible, like hiding in SAAHI

Todd's office and giving her brother an excuse to gloat at her expense.

She let Zeke out at her mother's condo and sat for a moment trying to make sense of things. In spite of her distress, she stifled one yawn after another, finally succumbing to one so powerful it made her eyes water. By the time she pulled into the rectory garage, she could hardly hold her head up. Leaving a note for her father to wake her at 6 to fix dinner, Petra slowly climbed the stairs and crawled into bed with all her clothes on.

* * *

She awoke disoriented. The green digits of the clock on her nightstand glowed 2:12. A hall light burned, but the rest of the house was dark. It made creaking noises like old houses do in the dead of night. Petra swung her legs out of bed, pleasantly surprised that they didn't lock with pain.

On a TV tray in the hall she found a peanut butter sandwich and a glass of lemonade, both covered with plastic wrap. On the sandwich lay a note. "Didn't have the heart to wake you. Please give a shout if you need me. Love, Dad."

Touched by her father's thoughtfulness, Petra carried the food to her room, gobbled it down, and went back to bed. She didn't wake again until nearly 11. Then, alarmed that she'd missed her early classes, she dashed around getting ready for school before it occurred to her that her flare-up was over at last. Really over. She could move freely again. She didn't hurt anywhere. Not much, anyway. And she brimmed with energy as she showered and dressed.

Petra glided downstairs a new person. Her father had opened the drapes to a gray day. The weather couldn't get her down, though. She breakfasted on toast and orange juice, relishing the return of her appetite, and washed all the dishes in the sink.

Fairly skipping out of the house, she threw her backpack and gym bag in her car and hurried across the lawn to the church.

"Well, my dear." Father Peter rose from his desk. "You astonish me. Do you feel as bright-eyed and bushy-tailed as you look?"

"Yep. See?" She lifted her arms over her head, touched her toes, and flexed each knee.

"Marvelous. Does it hurt anywhere?"

"Uh-uh." She wasn't pain-free, but ordinary soreness didn't count.

Reverend Elisabeth knocked on the open door. "May I come in?"

"Yes, yes, of course." Peter waved her in.

The young associate smiled at Petra. Flipping her ash-blond braid off her shoulder, she said, "It's wonderful to see you up and about, Petra. How are you?"

"Good, thanks."

"Glad to hear it. You've been in my prayers."

"Thank you." To her father Petra said, "I need an excuse for school."

"Will you be home straightaway?"

"Right after classes," Petra answered, mentally including her class at Master Lee's.

Elisabeth frowned. "That doesn't mean martial arts, I hope?"

Petra looked out the window at the church's overgrown memorial garden. Who did Reverend Elisabeth think she was—her mother? "Don't worry about me. I'm fine," she said, taking the note from her father. She saw fresh concern in his eyes and blamed Elisabeth for butting into their affairs.

"Drop in for a visit anytime," the young priest told her on her way out. "I'm always happy to talk."

Petra pretended not to hear.

Rejoicing in health restored, she buckled herself into her Toyota and backed out of the garage. Although it had cooled overnight and rain spattered the windshield, she rolled down the window. The scent of apple blossoms wafted in. Everything in the yard and up and down the street looked fresh, green, vibrant with color. Life was good again.

When Petra scurried into Horseman's class just before the bell, Jamie passed her a folded piece of paper. "McD's after school?"

"Mais oui," Petra wrote back. She didn't need to be at Master Lee's until 4.

"You look a lot better than you did yesterday," Jamie observed later in the student parking lot.

"I am a lot better. See?" She flexed her joints for Jamie, as she had for her father.

"I woke up this morning feeling like myself again. No more inflammation."

"That rocks, Pet. Let's keep it that way." At Petra's car Jamie said, "Have you decided yet about Running Start?"

"Why? You think you might miss me after all?" Petra unlocked the doors and stowed her backpack.

Jamie shoved hers in, too. "Of course I'd miss you. That's not the point." She paused over Petra's gym bag. "What's this?" Her expression grew serious. "You're not going back to that place today!"

"What place?" Petra climbed in front.

Jamie got in and slammed her door. "Don't be coy."

"Coy?" Petra laughed. "Coy?"

"Yes, coy. It's a word. I had to look it up for a take-home test."

"I know it's a word. I just didn't think—"

"You didn't think I was smart enough to know it?"

Petra put the car in gear and twisted to back up. The clouds had blown over and it was warm again. Kids with spring fever swarmed everywhere, laughing, joking, giving each other friendly pushes. A couple of guys were playing Frisbee right behind her, and she had to concentrate on not hitting them.

Jamie leaned out the window and yelled, "Back off, jockos!"

The guys grinned and waved at her. Petra felt sure if *she'd* said anything, they'd have beat on her trunk or aimed the Frisbee at her head.

"I think you're very smart," Petra said. "And I'm totally impressed with how you do that." She gestured toward the two guys receding in her rear-view mirror.

"What? Get a couple of shit-for-brains out of the way? Easy. All you have to do is not care if they like you or not. Most of the time, they do anyway. The fools."

"Yeah, they like you. What's not to like?"

"Thank you, loyal fan club." Jamie attempted a bow from the waist, but her seat belt trapped her and she went, "Ugh!"

Petra laughed.

"So...where were we?" Jamie tugged on her belt. "Oh, yeah. Martial arts or Running Start. You pick."

"You mean to talk about? Okay. Running Start. No, I haven't made a decision, but I did discuss it with Mother and Daddy. Mother thinks I'd be stupid not to do it." Petra glanced at Jamie. "Sort of like you."

"Good woman. I always did like your mom."

"I like yours, too."

"Great, but what's that got to do with beans in Boston? That's something my mom says, by the way."

"Yeah, I know."

"I'm surprised you remember. You've been so busy knocking yourself out for Chas the spaz, we haven't seen much of you lately."

Petra sighed. "Let's not go there, okay?"

"Fine, but you'd better make up your mind about Running Start. The deadline's coming up."

"How do you know?" Petra signaled at McDonald's, found a parking space, and killed the engine.

"Well," said Jamie, "I thought I'd check it out for myself."

"Really? Running Start?"

"Why not? I told you I'd ditch high school if I could."

"You mean you can apply for the program? I thought you had to be picked for it."

"Turns out you can do either. I've got my name in for an alternate opening."

Petra eyed her. "You're hooking up with someone at BCC, aren't you?"

"What if I am? Hey, we've been sitting here in a hot car

while the birds poop on your windshield. You wanna go in?"

Petra opened her door. A breeze fluttered the poplars along the street and raised goose bumps on her arms. Inside McDonald's she shivered in the air con.

"You want me to get your sweater from the car?" Jamie asked.

"No, it's okay." Petra walked up to the counter, glad to see there weren't many other high school kids in the store yet. Mobs of people her own age made her nervous. She didn't need that now with her first lesson back at Master Lee's only a little over an hour away.

While Petra picked at the fries she'd ordered, Jamie treated her to a description of Lars, the latest college man she'd met riding city transit. A Viking god from Jamie's point of view, he sounded dull to Petra. But then any boy would seem dull with Chas so much on her mind. When she couldn't bear another word about her friend's hunk *du jour*, she said, "Heard anything more from the school board about your P.E. requirement?"

"Nope, but it won't matter if I claim one of those Running Start openings." Jamie helped herself to Petra's fries.

Petra refrained from saying *don't count on it*. Jamie had all kinds of street smarts and art smarts and boy smarts. But school smarts? Forget it. Petra stood and collected her trash. "Come on, I'll give you a ride to Starbucks."

"Thanks. You heading home?"

Petra braced herself for an argument. "No. Master Lee's." But Jamie didn't argue. In fact, she didn't say anything for the next ten minutes. When they arrived at the strip mall, Petra asked, "Are you mad at me?"

"Just disappointed."

"Well, don't be, okay? I have to do what I think is best, you know."

"I know." Jamie vaulted out of the car, snagged her stuff from the back seat, and disappeared into Starbucks.

Petra blew out a long breath. Obviously, Jamie disapproved of her returning to martial arts so soon. Her parents wouldn't be thrilled either if they knew. She hated acting against other people's expectations. It made her uneasy, like she'd been sneaking around or something.

Petra hauled her uniform out of her gym bag and locked up. SAAHI Todd wanted everyone to buy bags with Master Lee's insignia on them, but she hadn't gotten around to it yet. She stood outside the studio door, remembering how sick she got the last time she practiced hard. Maybe she should go home. What would be so terrible about putting off her test for third section?

"You comin' or goin'?"

Petra whirled. She was so startled to see SAAHI Todd in street clothes that her jaw dropped. "Hello, Sawhee—that is...." She groped for words, unable for the life of her to remember what the initials stood for. Letting her uniform slip to the sidewalk, she executed a clumsy bow.

SAAHI Todd gazed down at the crumpled pile. "You been away so long you forgot your respect?" He reached for Petra's belt, which had uncoiled at his feet.

"Sorry." Petra dipped to retrieve her uniform at the same time and smacked heads with him. Abruptly, she sat down on the sidewalk.

SAAHI Todd grabbed his forehead. "Here, get up," he said, offering a hand.

Petra's arm twanged when he yanked on it, and her knees

cracked as she straightened up. She tried not to wince.

"Don't forget to bow to the flags." SAAHI Todd opened the glass door and pointed to his office.

"You mean I bow even when you're not there?"

"That's what I said." He held the door until she took it. Then he started down the hall toward the changing rooms.

"What about you?"

He pivoted. "Whaddaya mean?"

"Don't you bow to the flags, too?"

SAAHI Todd's dark eyes bored into hers. "Smart ass, ain't ya?" He stumped to the office beads, dropped his gym bag, and bowed.

"Yes, Seattle Area Associate Head Instructor Todd." Petra bowed to him when he turned around.

Halfway to the women's room Petra thought about seeing Chas again, and her knees went weak. She steadied herself against the wall and prayed that her training would take over during the lesson, because her nerves were shot.

Chapter 20

Heart thudding, Petra stepped through the beaded curtain into the practice room. She bowed to the flags and Instructor Franklin, the highest ranking person there. Of course her attention had gone straight to Chas.

He took his time acknowledging her presence. Something SAAHI Todd did often, but not Chas. Never before this. Petra's face burned with indignation by the time he quit correcting his mother's execution of a side kick and glanced up. He bowed without smiling and returned to Dee.

Petra made her lonely way to the mirrored wall and started warming up, her gaze on Chas's reflection. Evidently, he intended to slight her. Was this some kind of evil test devised by SAAHI Todd? Chas would never act so mean on his own. A little stiff from her week off, she practiced tai chi until Chas called his class of eight to order. Instructor Franklin took the children to the back of the room.

While Chas demonstrated a new self-defense maneuver, Petra studied his form, the way his arms and legs slid through the sequence of motions. She judged it wouldn't be a good idea for her to imitate him just yet. The action involved wrist-twisting and tumbling. As soon as she could beckon him aside, she told Chas her intention to stick to tai chi for a day or two, expecting him to agree.

To her complete and utter dismay, he said, "We decide what's best for you. Wimping out's not an option."

"I'm not wimping out!"

"Then take part in the lesson like everyone else." Chas moved away to critique the stance of a businessman he'd corralled on one of their visits to Starbucks.

Petra drew back. She'd never felt so misunderstood in her life. Part of the misunderstanding may have been her fault. She hadn't told Chas about her rheumatoid arthritis, and she doubted SAAHI Todd remembered their conversation about it. Still, Chas's callous words stung.

Cautiously, Petra rotated her wrist. Then she flicked it back and forth as if rattling bracelets. Not too much pain. Maybe she could do the exercise.

When Chas instructed them to pair up, Petra scooted to Dee's side.

"You must be feeling better." Dee's voice sounded scratchy.

"I was." Petra rolled her eyes toward Chas. "Until our instructor told me not to wimp out."

Dee shook her head. "I need to talk to that boy. I don't like to see him getting so caught up in Seattle Area Associate Head Instructor Todd's notion of a martial arts guru. It doesn't suit him." She sniffed, grabbed a tissue from her belt, and blew her nose.

Petra appreciated hearing her own view of Chas endorsed by his mother. "How's your cold?" she asked.

"*It's* great. *I* feel rotten." Dee tucked the used Kleenex into the other side of her belt. "Sorry about the germs." She rubbed her hands together. "They say friction kills the little buggers. Let's hope so."

"No problem," said Petra. "My immune system's so revved up, I hardly ever get viruses."

"Really? What'd you have last week, then?"

Petra saw Chas staring at them from the front of the group. "Shhh," she warned, bobbing her head in his direction.

Dee turned around, and Chas explained how he wanted them to do the new self-defense movement, demonstrating with one of the men. Out of the corner of her eye, Petra glimpsed SAAHI Todd at the side entrance to his office. Watching her, just like he said he would.

"I'll be careful," Dee promised as she and Petra faced off to practice.

"Me, too," said Petra. She and Dee pantomimed the throws, and no one got hurt.

During a free period, Petra worked more on her tai chi. She yearned for Chas to comment on her form, which was quite good, considering she'd been out of practice for more than a week. But he didn't. Once she sneaked a peek at SAAHI Todd's office through the mirror. She couldn't tell if he continued to watch or not.

As the session wound down in stretching drills, Petra felt pleased with the way she'd handled her first day back. But Chas's disapproving attitude worried her. Did it mean he saw things differently? Would he and SAAHI Todd decide she needed a full month more before she could test for third section?

After the others exited the room, Petra approached Chas. She cleared her throat and plunged in. "Do you have time for Starbucks?"

He regarded her distantly. "What?"

"Starbucks. Do you—I mean, would you...?" Petra's cheeks flamed. Chas made it so hard. "Have I done something wrong? I thought we were friends."

"Friends don't let friends goof off, Petra."

"What do you mean?"

"I mean we—Seattle Area Associate Head Instructor Todd and I—have invested a lot in you, putting you on the fast track to earn your black belt. We had high hopes for you to teach. You messed up."

"I didn't mess up. I got sick. I still want to do my black belt as fast as I can. And I want to teach with you. More than anything."

"Show me."

"What?"

"Show me—show us—you're serious about martial arts. Get back into practice. Work hard. Believe in Master Lee. You won't be sorry." Chas stepped away from her, his stern expression forbidding any argument. "Time for you to bow out."

Too stunned to do anything but obey, Petra stepped backward, bowed to Chas, then to the flags, and stumbled into the corridor. She flopped down by the water cooler, not ready to face the women in the changing room.

What did she have to do to prove herself around here? Walk on water? Rise from the dead? She fumed, her emotions dipping and swaying like a roller coaster. One second she wanted to tell Chas off for being so unfair, the next to beg his forgiveness. He did have a point, she supposed. Petra had quit believing in Master Lee when the symptoms of her flare-up didn't disappear right away. She'd reverted to waiting out the illness as she'd done in the past instead of contacting her instructors for direction. What about the sign she'd noticed on her first visit here? "All things are possible." *All* things, not just what doctors think is possible. Maybe Chas had it right. She really hadn't stuck with the program long enough to find out what it could do for her.

"Are you okay?"

Petra looked up. Dee stood over her, her dark blond hair damp and straggly. She had changed clothes, but her face glistened with sweat.

"I'm fine." Petra heaved herself up. Her hip and knee joints popped. "In fact..." She took a deep breath. "I'm going to be even better. Every day better and better."

After a moment Dee said, "Good—I think."

"Chas was right. I have to keep going, keep believing, keep working. I'm gonna be the best I can be from now on. No holding back."

"You sure you're okay?"

Petra mustered a smile. "Sure. I'm going back in to practice some more."

Dee shifted a red canvas carryall to her other shoulder. "I think there's something I should tell you first."

"What?"

"You know yesterday when I came in to sweat out my cold? It's worse than ever." She turned aside to sneeze. "I'm going home to bed, and I won't be back till I'm well." She fumbled in her bag for a tissue.

"What will Chas say about that?"

"Not much. I am his mother, after all." Dee's laugh ended in a loose cough.

"Are you saying you don't believe in Master Lee? I mean in what he says about all things being possible?"

"I'm saying I tried my best, and I still have a cold. I don't know what you had, honey." Dee paused, waiting for Petra to supply an explanation.

But Petra didn't want to give that much power to her RA. She wanted to overcome it with Master Lee's help.

Dee laid a hand on Petra's arm. "Whatever it was, I know you weren't faking. I've never seen anyone—other than my son—who's more enthusiastic about martial arts than you are."

Gratitude welled in Petra's chest. Why couldn't Chas and SAAHI Todd see what Dee could see? "Thanks," she said.

"Take care, honey. And listen to your body. You know more about what you need than Chas does. Or Seattle Area Associate Head Instructor Todd." Sniffing and wiping her nose, she headed down the hall.

Petra walked over to the beaded curtain. SAAHI Todd suspended his own practice to bow her in. A couple of students from her class were doing self-defense together. She went to the mirror, determined to run through every movement she'd learned at least twice. She would work out the kinks in her form and in her body, pushing through pain, fatigue, whatever her disease dished out.

She would show SAAHI Todd—and Chas—just what she was made of.

* * *

Petra worked hard the rest of the week, demonstrating her total commitment to martial arts and Master Lee's philosophy. At the end of the week, SAAHI Todd told her she could test for third section the following Tuesday. Standing at the beaded curtain to the office, Chas congratulated her for making up for lost time.

"Thank you, Assistant Instructor Chas." Petra bowed to him—she'd already bowed to SAAHI Todd—and backed away, professional to the core. No one would fault her again on anything. Not her dedication, not her form, not her etiquette.

On Sunday she stopped at a prayer station after Holy Communion to request healing for her joints, which were so sore she had to consciously avoid limping. Her faith in Master Lee had waned again and she felt the need of a Higher Power. But when Reverend Elisabeth approached the circle, Petra shuffled back to her pew. She couldn't admit how much she hurt to her father's associate. Elisabeth didn't understand. No one did, except Chas and the other people who took Master Lee seriously.

The next day Petra slipped into the high school's administrative wing before classes and left a note for the guidance counselor who'd offered her a place in the Running Start program. "After talking to both my parents," it read, "I've decided to do my junior and senior years here at Belville High. But thank you for considering me."

What a relief to have that out of her hair! Her parents and Jamie might disagree with her choice, but she'd finally made it. She would earn her black belt and teach at Master Lee's. Her relationship with Chas would deepen over time. That, not early college, was her destiny.

After school, while Zeke had his lesson, Petra practiced. She focused on the most difficult *katas,* losing herself in the quest to perfect her form. The kids finished their lesson. She practiced on. Sweaty and exhausted, she finished with rounds of *bagwa* walk in which she marched in a tight circle, knees bent and arms extended in readiness for combat. Then she sank against the back wall, feet thrust out in front of her, and began the *qigong* meditation she'd been taught to reenergize herself. Her body ached, but she breathed through the pain. In and out, breathing into the pain, ignoring the discomfort.

She opened her eyes and saw Chas looking at her. He quickly resumed his own practice, but she had been more than rewarded by his attentive gaze.

However, when Petra attempted to stand, her knees buckled and she fell back with a gasp. Glancing around to see if anyone had heard her, she groped the wall for balance, staggered to her feet, and careened toward the beaded curtain. Chas bowed her out with a smile, either unaware of her difficulties or glad to see she'd pushed through them.

It took forever to change clothes, every twist of her arm, every bend of her knee bringing fresh pain. Zeke sent a girl from his class to see what held her up. Petra emerged at last with a grin pasted on her face. Mind over matter. All things are possible.

On the slow walk to SAAHI Todd's office, she bumped into Chas at the corner. They bowed, and he said, "You got a minute?" He crooked a finger, and she trailed him back to the water cooler, flattered at being singled out. Maybe she had earned a private word of encouragement. Maybe he and SAAHI Todd had decided to test her now instead of making her wait till tomorrow.

"You know the junior prom is Saturday," Chas began without preliminary.

Petra's pulse thundered in her ears. All she could do was nod and say, "Uh-huh."

"Would you like to go?"

Would she like to go? Petra could have burst into the Hallelujah Chorus. "I'd love to," she said, her imagination leaping ahead to the weekend. Five days to shop and do her hair. Her first dance since middle school.

"Good. I'll pick you up at six."

"Six is great. Do you know where I live? St. Julian's rectory."

"I'll find it. See you later." Chas disappeared into the men's room.

Petra floated to SAAHI Todd's office, oblivious of Zeke fidgeting at the door, oblivious of her aching joints, oblivious of everything except Chas's invitation, still ringing in her ears.

"You dork," Zeke said as they approached Petra's car, "you forgot to put up the sun shield. It'll be roasting inside."

Petra refused to let the unseasonable heat or her bratty brother bring her down. She had to climb into her low-slung convertible in two stages: falling sideways onto the seat, then manually lifting her knees inside. Yet it seemed to her that she moved more fluidly by the minute. Master Lee had been right about the power of positive thinking. Sometimes it even yielded unexpected bonuses.

She put the car in gear, switched on the air conditioning, and backed out humming under her breath.

Zeke looked at her. "What are you so stoked about?"

"Wouldn't you like to know?" Petra would have told him, but he let out a snort.

"Like I care," he said.

"You asked."

"Only 'cause I know, and I thought I should warn you."

"Warn me about what?" Petra pulled into traffic.

"I heard Seattle Area Associate Head Instructor Todd tell Assistant Instructor Chas to take you out."

"What?" Petra slammed on her brakes. The driver behind blared his horn. Of all the outrageous things to say! Zeke had gone too far this time, and Mother would hear about it.

"Hey, doofus," yelled Zeke, "you wanna get us killed?"

"It's your fault for teasing me while I'm driving." Petra mouthed an apology to the offended driver through her rear-view mirror and motioned him past.

"I'm tellin' you the truth."

"I don't believe you."

Zeke shrugged. "That's your problem."

Petra's stomach churned, but she forced herself to pay attention to the road. "You must have misunderstood."

"I didn't. I got tired of waiting for you and I went outside for a while. When I got back, I saw Assistant Instructor Chas standing outside Seattle Area Associate Head Instructor Todd's office. I heard Chas—I mean Assistant Instructor Chas—say, 'She's doing really well. Better than I expected.' Then I heard Seattle Area—"

"Call him Sawhee," said Petra.

"Why?"

"It's shorter. S-A-A-H-I are the initials of his title."

Zeke considered. "I don't think he'd like that."

"I know he wouldn't, but it saves time. Go on." Petra tightened her grip on the steering wheel.

"Anyway, Seattle Area Associate Head Instructor Todd said, 'Ain't you got a dance or something you could take her to?'"

Petra's heart missed a beat, and she swallowed painfully. "This isn't funny, Zeke. If this is your idea of a joke...." She stopped for a light and faced her brother.

"It's the truth. I swear."

"What did Chas say?"

"He said, 'Sure, I'll ask her right away.'"

"But what *for*?" Petra couldn't keep her voice from rising to a wail. "Why would Sawhee Todd care whether Chas asks me out or not?"

"I dunno. I just thought you'd want to know."

Hardly. Her whole day had been spoiled. Petra crept forward through the green light as dazed as if she'd been sideswiped by an SUV. She didn't speak again until they arrived at their mother's condo. By then she'd sorted her feelings enough to conclude that, if Zeke was sincere about what he'd heard, he didn't have the whole story. Chas had probably mentioned his interest in dating Petra to SAAHI Todd, and SAAHI Todd must have put his seal of approval on it.

She hated knowing the head instructor had interfered in their relationship, but she had to accept Chas's respect for the chain of command, especially if, as Dee said, Chas considered SAAHI Todd a father figure. A hierarchy existed at the school, just as in the Episcopal Church. Although Petra doubted Daddy would have consulted with his bishop the first time he asked Mother out.

Zeke grabbed his gym bag and the dirty backpack at his feet.

"Don't take no wooden nickels," he said and jumped to the pavement, slamming the door behind him.

"What's that supposed to mean?" Petra yelled after him, but he didn't look back.

She put the car in gear and drove home, barely conscious of the ache in her hips and shoulders. She forced herself to face facts. If Zeke told the truth and Chas had acted on SAAHI Todd's instructions, she couldn't do much about it. Besides, whether SAAHI Todd suggested it or not, Chas himself had asked her to the prom. Why shouldn't she go with him? She would go anywhere with Chas.

And no one—least of all her infuriating little brother—would stop her.

Chapter 21

Petra rolled out of bed Tuesday with a sharp cry. Her hips were locked. When she put weight on her feet, her knees crumpled. She made a grab for her nightstand, which tipped its contents, including a glass of water, onto the floor. Okay, don't panic, she told herself. Think healthy, be healthy.

It hurt so much to pick up the glass and her digital clock that she decided to drop a towel over the rest of the mess and clean it up later. She had to conserve her energy for showering, dressing, and creeping downstairs, one jarring step at a time.

Although she skipped breakfast, Petra got to school ten minutes late and needed an excuse for tardiness. The nurse wanted to send her home. "You need to rest," she said after taking Petra's temperature and blood pressure.

Petra shook her head. "I'll be all right, but could I just wait here until my second class starts?" She didn't like the idea of hobbling into the middle of first period, drawing everyone's attention to her snail-like movements.

The nurse gave her reluctant approval. By lunchtime Petra was feverish and sick to her stomach.

"You look awful!" Jamie sprang off their bench to meet her. "Your face is all white except for two red spots, and you've got huge dark circles under your eyes." She seized one of Petra's icy hands and chafed it until Petra cringed with pain. Jamie frowned. "Here, let me take that." She helped Petra out of her backpack. "I'm driving you home. You must have been mental to come to school today."

"I had to come. I'm testing for third section this afternoon."

"Oh, no, you're not."

Petra didn't have the strength to argue. Besides, if Jamie took her home, she might sleep until 3:30 and be in better shape for the test. She simply couldn't wimp out again. Chas would never forgive her. She waited on the bench, shivering in the hot sun, while Jamie got permission to leave campus. Then she leaned on her friend all the way to the car. It was a long walk, and Petra collapsed into the passenger seat with her head back and her eyes closed. Jamie drove in silence.

When Petra had gathered enough ambition to speak again she said, "Guess what. Chas asked me to the junior prom yesterday."

"Shut up! You're serious?"

"Yep."

Seconds ticked by before Jamie said, "I'm happy for you, Pet. Really, I am. You have to admit, though, this isn't like the Chas we know."

You mean it isn't like the Chas *you* know, Petra thought. Aloud she said, "A person can change, can't he?"

"I guess." Jamie kept her eyes on the road.

"Will you shop with me?" asked Petra.

"Absolutely, if you're up to it. If not, I'll bring some of my formal dresses over for you to try on."

"That's nice, Jamie. I wasn't sure how you'd feel about—you know—Chas taking me out."

"What do you mean?"

"I know you don't like him."

"True, but I like it that he's interested in you, not just in what you can do for Master Lee's."

Petra hesitated, remembering Zeke's latest disclosure. "Master Lee's doesn't need me."

"Of course they do. You said so yourself. You told me they'd lost their female instructor and wanted you to take her place."

"Yes, but...." Chas wouldn't date her just to snare another employee for SAAHI Todd. How ridiculous.

"They don't pay, you know," said Jamie. "Master Lee's expects assistant instructors to work for free."

"What? How do you know that?"

"It's one of the first things Chas told me about himself. He doesn't even realize they're taking advantage of him. He says the payoff is that they'll set him up to run one of Master Lee's schools after he graduates."

Petra received this news without comment, but her feelings were far from quiet. Chas worked for free? Chas expected *her* to work for free? She couldn't think about it now. Her brain fogged. Petra lay against the headrest, surrendering to the hypnotic hum of tires on pavement.

"Here we are," Jamie announced.

Petra roused with a start. They had turned onto the rectory's bumpy gravel driveway. "Thanks for bringing me home, Jamie. How will you get back to school?"

"Bus stop down the road." Jamie parked the car in the garage next to Father Peter's Mini.

"I'll ask Dad to drive you."

"Great. Now hold on till I get around to your door."

Petra couldn't face the climb to her bedroom, so she curled up on the sofa. Jamie tucked an afghan around her and ran upstairs for Petra's pillow.

"I threw that wet towel in the bathtub and put your nightstand stuff back," said Jamie, plumping the pillow.

"Thanks. I was in a hurry this morning. Would you hand me the phone so I can call Dad?"

Afterward, Jamie flitted around placing everything Petra might need within arm's reach. Petra's eyelids grew heavier and heavier. The bustle of activity faded. Later she couldn't remember if she said goodbye to Jamie or not. She barely noted her father's entrance and the two of them speaking in hushed tones.

"I'm going to ring the doctor, my dear." Her father held her hand.

Petra stirred. "No, don't. Please don't."

The next thing she knew, her hand lay under the afghan, still freezing cold, like her feet. She heard Peter on the phone until she drifted off. If the doctor came, she'd just tell Petra to sleep anyway. Might as well get on with it.

* * *

Petra awoke to the eerie sound of moaning—her own

moaning, she realized with a shock. Her face was hot and her mouth tasted like she'd thrown up. Somewhere nearby people were talking and moving about. She smelled something repugnant yet familiar, a cross between antiseptic and body odor.

Prying open her eyes, she struggled to identify her surroundings. A flimsy curtain to her right, an IV pole and monitors to her left, a bedside tray, dull green walls. She flexed her hand and felt the tug of the IV needle.

"What time is it?" Her words slurred thickly. No matter. No one to hear them. She fell back into a fitful sleep and dreamed her family visited her in the hospital. In the dream her father told the nurses to make Petra well because he intended to take her home.

Later she opened her eyes again. The curtain had been drawn between her bed and the next. Reverend Elisabeth sat on a metal folding chair reading a book. She wore a gray clerical blouse and collar with a gray skirt that strained across her middle. Her wispy ashen hair had lost its braid and had been tied back with a dark ribbon.

Petra didn't want to talk to her, so she pretended to sleep. After what felt like twenty or thirty minutes, Petra peeked. Elisabeth hadn't budged, but Petra was too restless to keep pretending. "What are you doing here?" she demanded, aware that she sounded rude yet unwilling to fake pleasantries.

Reverend Elisabeth set aside her book and smiled. "Well, hello there, sleeping beauty. How do you feel?"

"Mouth's dry. I want something to drink."

Elisabeth got up and whisked a glass of water from the tray. "They put a straw in it for you." She held it to Petra's lips.

Petra slurped most of it down. "How long have I been here? Where's Dad?" She tipped her head toward the curtain. "Is someone over there?"

Elisabeth nodded. "A woman scheduled for surgery. They took her for tests." She scraped her chair forward. "Your dad brought you in last night."

"Last night! What time is it now?"

Elisabeth checked her watch. "About three in the afternoon. Your father was here until noon. Your mom and brother came to visit this morning. Oh, and your friend Jamie called a few minutes ago. I said I'd let her know when you're up to talking."

Tears sprang to Petra's eyes. How could she have slept a whole day away? She'd missed her test. SAAHI Todd would be furious. Chas's disappointment in her would be unbearable.

"Did anyone else call?" she asked. Maybe, if they knew at Master Lee's about her hospitalization, they'd realize it was out of her hands.

"Not that I know of," said Elisabeth.

"Oh."

But what if Chas *had* called and Elisabeth wouldn't tell her because she disapproved of him, disapproved of Petra's involvement in martial arts? Petra was still angry at herself for confiding so much to the young priest before she started at Master Lee's. Elisabeth had obviously confused Chas with one of her own boyfriends, James somebody, who'd broken her heart. Because of her bad experience with James, she couldn't see Chas or Petra's sense of destiny about him in a clear light.

Petra looked hard at her father's associate, hoping to make her squirm if she held anything back.

Elisabeth stood. "Are you in pain?"

"No, are you?"

Elisabeth cocked her head quizzically. "Me in pain?"

"Never mind." Tentatively, Petra bent one knee. "Hey, it doesn't hurt!" She wriggled onto her side and saw that she'd been catheterized. "I don't need this thing. Tell them to take the tubes out of me." She jerked on the catheter, then the IV cord.

"Not so fast." Elisabeth's hands flew out, but she stopped short of restraining Petra. "You need that stuff."

"No, I don't. I feel fine."

"Your father told me they put you on intravenous steroids and that they'd be taking effect sometime this afternoon."

"Steroids?" Petra pulled herself to a sitting position and tried to rearrange the pillows to support her back—a frustrating exercise because her shoulder joints were frozen. The effort to get comfortable again left Petra panting with fatigue, but she resented Elisabeth's hovering over her, offering to help. She didn't need help. She needed out of this place.

"Here, let me crank that up for you." Elisabeth found the button to raise the head of the bed. "Better?" When Petra settled back with a grudging nod, Elisabeth continued, "The drug has a long name, but it's related to prednisone, which Peter said you took orally for some time after your last hospitalization."

Petra looked away. She wasn't well after all. Just medicated.

Elisabeth seemed to read her mood. "It had to be done." She smoothed Petra's blanket. "Your inflammation had gotten out of control. You were delirious. Peter said you were burning up with fever until they started the IV. Hang on, though. I'll get a nurse to talk to you."

When Elisabeth returned with a doctor instead and joined Petra in lobbying for removal of the tubes, Petra relented toward her a little. Unhooked at last, she used the bathroom and toddled down the hall a few feet to test her strength. Not bad for a wimp. If Chas could see her now, would he unbend or would he label her a hopeless wus?

Elisabeth watched her back into bed and reseated herself in the folding chair. Petra coped with the demands of general conversation while her thoughts remained tethered to Chas. Did he know about her hospitalization? Would he believe how sick she'd been? Once or twice she caught herself wondering if he was worth all the misery she'd been through the last two months. But then she would remember his long-lashed amber eyes, that angelic look on his face in the coffee shop, his invitation to the prom, and she'd melt inside.

"Elisabeth?" Petra hated to do it, but she had to talk to someone. "Do you think it's possible to care and still not call or visit when a friend is sick?"

Elisabeth uncrossed her legs to scoot closer to Petra's bed. "Sure, it's possible," she said. "People get busy. Things come up. You have to take a person's actions in context. Weigh them against everything else he or she has done."

"What if they do it more than once? I mean, what if they're under orders or something?"

"Orders?"

"You know, like a vow of silence. A kind of religious vow." Petra felt her way into this scenario as she spoke. Early on, Jamie had compared Chas's reverence for Master Lee's school to her father's reverence for the church. Things Petra had been unable to accept before suddenly came into focus around this realization. It wasn't that Chas didn't care. Rather, SAAHI Todd had forbidden him from contacting her while she was sick. Chas must be in anguish, trying to find a way around his superior's demands.

"I'm not sure what you mean," said Elisabeth. "Was there anyone in particular you had in mind? Anything you want to talk about?"

Petra shook her head. Better to quit while she had something positive to hold onto. Elisabeth's words had reminded her that she'd worried about this before, but Chas had eventually come around. He'd even asked her to a dance. Of course he cared.

"Thanks, anyway. You helped me a lot."

Elisabeth eyed her curiously but didn't push for an explanation.

By the time Peter showed up during dinner, which Petra didn't eat because the food tasted bland, the doctor had signed her discharge papers. Catherine and Zeke came soon after that. Petra was so glad to see them all, she even hugged her brother.

While the family waited outside, a big man with dark skin and long black hair parted down the center assisted Petra into a wheelchair. Perching on the edge of the bed, he handed her a list of instructions.

Petra glanced at them before asking, "Are you a doctor?" The one who'd checked her out earlier was a woman.

"Nope, I'm a physician's assistant. But I've got the doctor's orders right here." He riffled the pages of her chart. "Let's see. Make an appointment with your rheumatologist to monitor meds. Take oral prednisone daily with food until your doc says to taper off. And play hooky tomorrow." He glanced up with a grin.

"Tomorrow only?" Petra sat forward. "It's okay to go back to school Friday? And it's okay to do other things after that?"

"Depends how you feel. And it depends on what you have in mind when you say *other things*." He shook his finger with mock severity. "I hear you're a Jackie Chan wannabe. That's out."

Petra moistened her lips. "For how long?"

"At least the rest of this week. After that, ask your doc, okay?"

"What about—" She saw her family at the door and lowered her voice. She didn't want the woman beyond the curtain to hear, either. "What about a dance on Saturday?"

The PA grinned. "Hot date, huh?"

Petra shifted her gaze.

"Well, I don't see the harm." He winked. "Just the slow dances, though."

She beamed at him. For a moment she considered kissing him full on the mouth, but she was a clergyman's daughter, after all.

Best to save her lips for Chas.

Chapter 22

Petra followed doctor's orders and stayed home Thursday, avoiding martial arts altogether. She wouldn't even pull her dirty uniform out of the gym bag to wash it. When she returned to school on Friday, Petra didn't see Chas, which put her in an awkward position. Was their date still on? Had he forgotten? She pushed the troublesome thought from her mind.

Jamie went shopping with her after school, and they picked out a satiny dress in sea-foam green that accented her eyes. Petra also bought new shoes, earrings, and a matching bracelet. She didn't tell Jamie she hadn't heard from Chas since he asked her to the prom. Talking about it would only heighten her anxiety.

Saturday dawned sunny and warm. Petra, who hadn't slept well, threw off her covers and sat on the edge of the bed testing her flexibility. The prednisone hyped her up and gave her a funny puffy feeling, but she could move okay. The clock read 7:15. Less than eleven hours to go! If Chas didn't call by lunchtime, she would try to get hold of Dee. Phoning her would be less risky than talking to Chas himself.

Petra stood and stretched, then got into her robe almost as effortlessly as a healthy person. For breakfast she made pancakes from a mix, cut up fresh strawberries, and heated some maple syrup in the microwave. Her father dug in, making appreciative noises as he ate. Petra had thought she was hungry, but she couldn't get much down.

"Delicious," Peter said between bites. "But you're not eating. How do you feel?"

"A little nervous," Petra admitted. "The dance, you know."

"Ah, yes, the dance." Her father forked another pancake onto his plate. "You're certain you're up to all that activity?"

"Daddy!" Petra pushed her plate away with a frown. "Of course I'm up to it. This is my first prom. I spent a lot of money on a dress. No way am I gonna stay home."

"I didn't mean to upset you, my dear." Peter quit eating long enough to give her a reassuring glance.

"It's okay."

"What time will your young man be here, and what's his name again?"

"Chas." Petra straightened her silverware. "He said six."

"He's taking you to dinner, then. I'll just nip out for a spot of Chinese, shall I? Or would you like me to meet him?"

She nodded, unaware that her father had asked an either-or question. Had Chas made a restaurant reservation? Would there be candlelight and soft music? Her heart fluttered uncomfortably. Would there be anything at all? Maybe she should call Dee now.

"More coffee, Daddy?" Petra got up to refill his cup and scrape her food into the disposal.

"So I meet him first, then go for take-away?" Her father held out his cup. "I'm afraid I don't have much knowledge of teenage dating rituals. Perhaps you'd prefer that I—what's the expression?—lay low until later?"

"Whatever you want, Daddy." Petra heard impatience in her voice, but she felt too distracted to correct it. "Will you excuse me? I'm going back upstairs."

As she climbed, clinging to the banister, she broke into a sweat. Her pulse pounded. It might be her illness or her medication. More likely it was the prospect of phoning Dee. Chas should be at Master Lee's, but she remembered the last time she'd made that assumption.

Her finger poised over the OFF button of her cell, she flinched when someone answered.

"Hello?"

Petra relaxed. "Dee?"

"Yes, this is Dee LaGuardia."

"Hi, this is Petra Goodwyn. From Master Lee's."

"How are you, Petra?" Dee sniffled. "I've been down all week with this nasty cold."

"I'm fine now. I was in the hospital."

"Oh, no! A car accident?"

"No." Petra couldn't bring herself to name her disease. She settled for a partial truth. "Dehydration. I'm over it now."

"Good. That flu—or whatever it was—really hit you hard, didn't it? Makes me feel like a whiner with my poky little bug. But I'm glad you're recovering so well."

"Thanks." Petra drew a deep breath and plunged in. "Did you know Chas asked me to the junior prom?"

Dee hesitated. "No, I didn't. I'm glad, though. Chas seldom

does anything outside of martial arts. It'll do him good to go to a school function."

"The thing is," Petra blurted, "the dance is tonight, but I haven't seen him since Monday. I want to—you know—make sure he's coming when he said he would."

"Oh, I see. Hmm." Dee clicked her tongue. "I'd put him on, but he's at Master Lee's. Saturday classes and practice. Do you have his cell number?"

"No, that's okay. I wouldn't want to interrupt him at work." More precisely, she couldn't bear the thought of a rejection over the phone. If only she could talk to Chas like she talked to his mother. Suddenly recognizing a chance to follow up on something Jamie had told her, she asked, "Is it true Seattle Area Associate Head Instructor Todd doesn't pay his assistants?" Lest Dee think she wanted to pry into Chas's personal affairs, she added, "I'm just wondering because Chas says they're thinking of letting me teach after I earn my black belt."

"Fantastic, honey. You'd make a great teacher."

"Really? That's what Chas said."

"It's true. You're quick and smart. Dedicated, too." Dee stopped to cough and clear her throat. "It's also true about Seattle Area Associate Head Instructor Todd not paying his high-school assistants. You need rich parents if you want to work for him." She laughed, which stimulated another coughing fit. "I can't afford it myself, but Chas's father tries to make up to Chas for the divorce by showering him with material things. A generous allowance, private lessons, a classic car. Whatever Chas wants. Chas talks about paying him back when Master Lee puts him in charge of a new school, but I doubt Charles Senior will hold him to it."

"Mm."

Petra didn't realize she'd grown quiet until Dee spoke again. "Tell you what. I'll have Chas give you a buzz as soon as he gets home."

"Okay." Before Petra hung up she said, "I hope you get over your cold soon."

"Thanks, honey. Have fun tonight. Take lots of pictures, okay?"

Petra pocketed her phone, comforted by Dee's matter-of-fact manner, which made the date with Chas seem less uncertain. Now that she knew the secret of his financial status, she felt a little less intimidated by him, too. Of course she would never embarrass him by mentioning it. She hated that SAAHI Todd used his position of authority to get slave labor, though. She'd have to think long and hard about doing anything for him without compensation.

Petra went to the closet for her dress. She loved to run her fingers over the slippery folds. Trying it on for the tenth time with her new heels and jewelry, she analyzed the total effect in the full-length mirror on her door. Not bad, but her hair was dull. When she showered she would use more of that highlighting rinse Catherine had given her. She thought about making a trip to the salon to have it styled but decided she was too nervous to take Chas's call in public.

By 1:30, with lunch finished and cleared away, Petra wanted to pull her hair out, dull or not. What in the world would she do with herself until Chas got back to her? She wished she could practice. Hauling out her textbooks, she spread them on her desk. Nearly a week's worth of assignments to make up, but she couldn't concentrate. Her eyes kept roaming to the clock on her nightstand, and her mind insisted on drifting to Chas. Where was he now? When would he call?

It got to be 3:10, and her phone remained maddeningly silent. Should she ring his house again? Why hadn't she taken Chas's cell number from Dee? Anything—even Chas's fury—would be easier than this endless waiting. She watched the luminous digits of the clock stick forever on 3:11... 3:12... 3:13....

Petra was in the shower when the call came over the landline. Her father hollered to her through the bathroom door. She skidded in her rush to get out of the tub and smashed an elbow on the wall flinging a towel around her body. Her voice shook when she said hello.

"Petra, this is Chas LaGuardia."

She heard her father hang up downstairs. "Yeah. Hi, Chas." She turned her face away from the receiver so he couldn't hear her heavy breathing.

"I can't make it tonight. I'm sorry."

Petra slid to the floor, her heart slamming into her ribs.

"Petra? Are you there?"

"Why? Why can't you make it?"

Long pause. "It wasn't my idea in the first place."

Petra's stomach lurched. Zeke had been right. She should have prepared herself for this.

"I mean," said Chas, "I wasn't against it or anything. Seattle Area Associate Head Instructor Todd wanted to reward you for renewing your commitment to Master Lee's. We both did, actually. But after this week—"

Petra interrupted him. "I don't understand. Did you invite me to the dance or did Todd?" She took satisfaction in deliberately omitting SAAHI Todd's title.

"I did, but—"

"Did you want to go?"

"Sure. I'm not much of a dancer, but it would have been fun. It's just out of the question now."

Petra's head reeled. "I bought a new dress" was all she could say.

"I'm sorry," Chas said. "I really am."

"Then why are you doing this?"

"Seattle Area Associate Head Instructor Todd says that under the circumstances—that is, since you skipped your test for third section and we haven't seen you at the school since Monday—he can't allow me to take you out."

"*Allow* it! He controls your social life, too?"

"It's not a matter of control. Not the way you think. My whole life is ruled by my commitment to Master Lee's. Yours would be, too, but you've chosen your way over the way of the true martial artist."

"My way!" Petra exploded. "I've been sick. Doesn't anyone at Master Lee's get that?"

Chas didn't respond, and Petra imagined him tight-lipped, disapproving, superior. Well, she didn't care anymore. Chas was unfair. Chas wasn't his own person. Chas was SAAHI Todd's stupid robot. Jamie had him pegged from the beginning. How could she, Petra, have been such a fool?

"We can help you," Chas said. "You need to show up for lessons, though."

"Oh, pardon me," Petra shot back. "I forgot to ask someone at the hospital to wheel me down in an ambulance."

"An ambulance?"

"Yes, an ambulance. I stayed overnight at Belville Medical Center Tuesday. I'm sorry I didn't call about the test, but you see, I was kind of incapacitated. Unconscious, in fact."

"Unconscious? Were you in an accident?"

"Would it matter to you?"

"What do you mean? Of course it matters."

"Then, no, I wasn't in an accident. I was sick. I had a severe flare-up of a disease I've had since childhood. That's what happened the first time I missed lessons, too."

"I don't know what to say," Chas began. "Master Lee...."

Petra wanted to hurl the phone across the room. The strength of her rage frightened her. She forced herself to hold it in check as Chas spouted the no-pain, no-gain doctrine that had led her to ignore her own common sense and landed her in the hospital. Inhale, she told herself. Exhale. Slowly, slowly.

When she could speak, she said, "You have a big issue with illness, don't you, Chas? Well, for your information, so do I. I hate being sick. I have juvenile rheumatoid arthritis, and if you don't know what that is, look it up online. It's something Master Lee can't cure. I know, because I've tried. God knows I've tried."

Chas sighed. "Like I said, Petra, we can help you, but you have to believe, and you have to be willing to work hard. There isn't a whole lot I can do otherwise. I plan to make a career with Master Lee, and that means obeying higher belts."

"Wait a second—"

He kept talking. "Whether we like it or not, Seattle Area Associate Head Instructor Todd says you and I can't date till you get back on track at Master Lee's. It's no good taking a week off here and there. You can't advance that way. Whatever your problem is, you have to overcome it. If you're going to teach, you need to learn self-discipline, consistency, and respect for authority."

Petra couldn't believe her ears. Had Chas heard a single word she'd said? He sounded like he was reading from one of Master Lee's brochures.

"Do you care about me at all?" she asked when he paused for breath.

"What kind of question is that? You're the first girl—I mean, you're the only girl I've met who...." He faltered. "I'm just following orders. Don't blame me for this."

"But I do blame you, Chas LaGuardia! Who else can I blame? You asked me out. You're dissing me. You're making a choice."

"You don't understand. Look, my hands are tied until you come back to Master Lee's and do what the higher belts tell you to do."

Poor Chas, his hands were tied. What a loser. How could she have been so blind to him? He was like one of the weirdos in that psychology experiment who kept administering shocks of electricity to apparently helpless victims just because a scientist in a white coat told them to do it.

"You'll see," Chas continued. "Things will be good between us after this blows over. You'll test for third section and get back with the program. We'll be on the same page, working toward the same goal. Seattle Area Associate Head Instructor Todd will approve our relationship again, and I'll take you to the senior prom next year."

"I don't think so, Chas. Two's company, three's a crowd,

and you already have Master Lee." Before Petra could change her mind, she hung up, put her wet head in her hands, and let the storm break.

She cried until she couldn't cry anymore, until the tears turned to salt. She sobbed herself hoarse. Then she wiped her eyes on her bath towel and got off the floor, surprised at how clear she felt. Free of illusion, free of misguided efforts to prove something to Chas. To anybody.

After packing her dress and shoes back in their boxes, she dried her hair. It combed out golden brown and silky, and she made a mental note to buy more of that rinse.

If Chas couldn't appreciate it, someone else would. She would.

Chapter 23

"Don't you hate his guts?" Jamie asked. She and Petra lounged on their customary bench outside the school cafeteria. They'd finished lunch early and were enjoying the June sunshine. Chas had just given them a curt nod as he passed, prompting Jamie's question.

"I did for a while. Maybe I still do, a little." Petra nibbled a handful of raisins. "I don't want him anymore, though."

"I hate to say I told you so, but—"

"Then don't."

Jamie ducked her curly red-gold head. "Sorry. I can't get over what a jerk he was. Backing out of the dance just because Todd Almighty told him to."

Petra shrugged. "He did me a favor in a way."

"What favor?" Jamie's blue eyes widened.

"I was making myself sick trying to please him and Sawhee Todd. I love martial arts, but it's supposed to be fun—not send me to the hospital."

Jamie blew out a breath. "You don't know how glad I am to

hear you say that, Pet." She hesitated. "You haven't gone back, then?"

"To the hospital?"

"No, silly. To Master Lee's."

"Of course not."

"Because you're still too sick?"

"No, my doctor says I'm recoving well. She took me off prednisone—it's not meant for long-term use—and I'm getting weekly injections of a new drug that's supposed to balance my immune system." Petra glanced past the school buildings to the silver maples glittering green and white in the distance. A trio of girls dressed in pre-faded jeans, spaghetti-strap tops, and platform heels clumped in front of them.

"You feel okay on the new meds?"

"Not bad. So far the shots haven't given me stomachaches or mouth sores like the stuff I took after the last hospitalization. I have to be thankful for that, because the doctor said I may never have another remission like I had the last few years."

"Oh." Jamie appeared to choose her words with care. "Does she think it's because of martial arts overkill?"

"She doesn't, but I do. How could I not? Dr. Patel says rheumatoid arthritis is unpredictable, and it's different for everyone who has it. She told me it's important not to blame myself for my disease."

"It *is* important not to blame yourself. You couldn't know what would happen."

Petra cast Jamie a surprised look. "You mean that?"

"Sure."

"Even though you tried to warn me and I wouldn't listen?"

Jamie spread her hands. "Who listens to anybody when they know better? I wouldn't have listened, either."

"I didn't know better. I just thought I did."

"Same thing. I remember you were always talking about signs and answers to prayer. You did the best you could to pay attention. Who knows? Maybe your destiny required you to push the envelope. Give it all you had. Practice till you dropped."

"Stalk Chas till he dumped me?" Petra's mouth twisted in a wry smile.

"You didn't stalk him, Pet. And from everything you've told me, you dumped *him*."

"I suppose I did." Petra was thoughtful. "Mother would agree with you about the destiny part. She says some things can't be learned without experience, even if it's hard experience."

"She's right. She's your mother, after all." Jamie laughed. "You know I'm ecstatic that you've left that place. But don't you miss it? You were so…into it."

"I was, wasn't I?" Petra mused aloud, awed by her own capacity for grand passions. "I do miss it, to tell you the truth. I miss the sense of purpose, of driving toward a difficult goal. I miss the movements. I dream about them at night. I miss Dee, although we've talked a couple times on the phone. She apologized for Chas's rudeness and said she gave him a piece of her mind about it. For all the good it did." Petra made a face. "I even sort of miss Sawhee Todd. No one can mangle the English language quite like he does."

"Da dope ain't got no culture," Jamie said, perfectly mimicking Todd's accent. "Don't get me wrong now, but I'm curious. What keeps you from going back if it's not your RA?"

"You mean besides Chas? And the totally bizarre way he and Sawhee Todd live and breathe Master Lee?"

"Yeah, besides that."

Petra rolled her eyes. "Well, let's see. It might be that I can't be myself there. I'd never be safe, either. Even with written doctor's orders to wave under their noses. They have this philosophy, you know. Master Lee's way or the highway." She paused for effect, then grinned at Jamie. "Or maybe it's the call I got."

"The call? What call?"

"From Lateesha Briggs. She's the woman who helped me when I had that bad flare-up. Actually, I called her and she called me back."

"How come?" Jamie threw her backpack off the bench and propped her feet on it. "I mean why'd you call her in the first place?"

"I remembered she told me her brother belongs to a tai chi group that meets at the park."

"Oh, ho! Now we're getting somewhere. Tell me more."

"I went Saturday and met Darnell, Lateesha's brother. He's really nice. He showed me the way they do tai chi. It's different. A lot slower and more mindful than Master Lee's version."

"*He* showed you? Darnell, not the leader dude? They do have a leader dude, don't they?"

"Yeah, but I didn't see him. I got there after their practice."

"Mm-hmm." Jamie nodded wisely. "And you're sure your doc is okay with this?"

"You mean tai chi? Yeah. She says the slow forms are good for my joints."

"I bet that's not all that's good for you." Jamie tilted her head. "How old did you say this Darnell guy is?"

Petra couldn't hold Jamie's penetrating gaze. "I didn't say," she said, glancing away. "But he's seventeen, finishing up his freshman year at Belville Community College. He's going to introduce me to the tai chi teacher next time."

"Is he cute?"

"How do I know? I haven't met him yet."

Jamie aimed a playful slap at Petra's knee. "Darnell, goofy girl."

Petra tried to suppress the smile that bubbled up.

"Aha!" Jamie swung her legs off her backpack. "No wonder you're recovering so well from Chas the spaz. I bet you've changed your mind about Running Start, too."

"As a matter of fact, I have," said Petra. "I talked to my advisor last week."

"What? You're not gonna graduate with me?"

Petra rounded on her. "Come on, Jamie! You're the one who lectured me about passing up a great chance to get my first two years of college at the same time I finish my last two years of high school."

"Just kidding." Jamie put up her hands as if to ward off blows. "You may as well know, I didn't make it out of the gate on Running Start. Got the notice in the mail over the weekend. *We take smart people. Others need not apply.*"

"Oh, Jamie, they didn't say that."

"Not in so many words. Anyway, I'm not as pissed about hanging out here for another two years as I might have been if I hadn't won my appeal with the school board. It won't be so bad if I don't have to give up art and music for P.E."

"Yeah, that's cool. Way to go."

Jamie saw her watch. "Well, Pet. Looks like it's about that time."

"We still have a few more minutes. I'm not ready to be cooped up yet."

"Fine with me." Jamie leaned against the bench. "Besides, there's something I want to ask before I forget. Did you get a refund on the dress?"

"Yeah." Petra sighed. "Shoes, too. I hated taking them back, they were so pretty."

"Oh, well." Jamie wiggled her eyebrows. "Next year with Darnell. We'll buy you something even more glam."

"Come on. I hardly know the guy."

"Yet. By the way, is Zeke still taking lessons at Master Lee's?"

"Yeah."

"Who drives him?"

"*Moi*, who else?"

"That's harsh. How do you stand it?"

"I don't go in. I just drop him off and pick him up. I figure he'll find out eventually what kind of place it is."

"But doesn't it bother you to hear him talk about Chas and watch him earn his belts and all?"

"Yes, yes, yes! It bothers me, all right? It makes me totally nauseous. But why should Zeke quit just because I did?"

"Why not invite him to the new place?"

"I will, after I go myself and see what it's like. This time I'm really going to check it out. Make sure it's right for me. I hope to take a friend along to help."

"Who, me?"

"Sure, if you're interested. But I meant someone who has a black belt already."

"Not Chas!"

Petra groaned. "Give me a break, Jamie. I said a *friend*. She's...a new friend. It took me a while to warm up to her."

"Well, who is it? Darnell's sister—what's her name, LaToya?"

"Lateesha. No, it's Reverend Elisabeth, my dad's associate."

"Oh." Jamie's face fell. "She has a black belt?"

"Yeah, in aikido. She also has a sister with RA. Elisabeth spent a lot of time with me in the hospital, and later she listened while I bawled my eyes out over Chas."

"I would have listened, too, you know. But you kept your feelings to yourself. At least you didn't share them with me."

"I know, I know." Petra thought about how to frame what she had to say. "It's just that I was super hurt and embarrassed. I had a lot to sort out. Elisabeth doesn't know Chas, and she was right next door at the church. I guess I felt more comfortable talking to her anyway." Petra stared at her sandaled feet. "I hated to admit you were right about him. I didn't want to hear *I told you so*."

Jamie grew quiet.

Petra nudged her with an elbow. "Hey, you're still my best friend. Nothing's gonna change that."

Jamie crossed her arms over her chest. When Petra didn't say anything more, she said, "Not even leaving Belville High?"

"Especially not that."

"Good, 'cause I won't have time to find a new best friend."

"More hours at Starbucks?"

"Nope. New hookup."

"Oh, jeez, I should have known." Petra smacked her forehead with the palm of her hand. "You have that glow. What's his name?"

"Darnell. He's seventeen, finishing his freshman year at BCC."

Petra's mouth fell open. Then she saw the gleam in her friend's eye. "Oh, you!"

Jamie laughed. "Gotcha. Really, his name's Stephen, and he goes to the U."

"Fine," said Petra. "You stay away from Darnell, and I'll stay away from Stephen. Deal?"

"Deal." Jamie stuck out a hand to shake. "Except if we double date."

"Unlikely."

"Why?"

Petra hoisted herself off the bench. "Because you'll be going out with someone else before Darnell and I have a chance to get to know each other."

"Not this time," said Jamie. "This one's the real deal."

Petra snorted. "That's what you always say." She shouldered her book bag. "Time for class."

Jamie grabbed her pack and followed Petra. "Just think." She lingered outside the building. "Only three more days of Horseman, counting today."

"Now that's what I call good news." Petra reached for one of the double entry doors. A strange feeling stirred in her chest—half excitement, half nostalgia. After Wednesday she would never cross this threshold again. Never have occasion to walk the halls of Belville High or share gossip with Jamie over a brown-bag lunch.

"Onward and upward," said Jamie.

"Horseward." Petra waited for Jamie's whinny. When it came, she laughed and they went inside.

About the Author

Judy Dearborn Nill is the author of several young adult novels, including *Just for Kicks*, *Simple Twists of Faith*, and *The Rise and Fall of Bibi Karstad.* She worked as a journalist, a college instructor, and a therapist before opening her private practice in counseling. She and her husband live in the Seattle area.

Made in the USA
Lexington, KY
08 April 2011